AUTUMN AT THE OAK LEAF CAFE

CP WARD

BY CP WARD

The Delightful Christmas Series

I'm Glad I Found You This Christmas

We'll have a Wonderful Cornish Christmas

Coming Home to Me This Christmas

Christmas at the Marshmallow Cafe

Christmas at Snowflake Lodge

Christmas at Log Fire Cabins

A Stranger Arrives this Christmas

A Train is Late This Christmas

The Glorious Summer Series

Summer at Blue Sands Cove

Summer at Tall Trees Lake

Summer at Harbour View House

The Warm Days of Autumn Series

Autumn in Sycamore Park

Autumn at the Willow River Guesthouse

Autumn in Sunset Harbour

Autumn at the Oak Tree Cafe

AUTUMN AT THE OAK LEAF CAFE

1

COMING HOME

Madeline Fellow's train was three hours late.

What should have been a relatively straightforward two and a half hours of reading a generic airport paperback turned into a near six-hour marathon, exactly what Madeline hadn't wanted from her first day back in England in more than two years. However, despite being far from the ideal start, it had been made semi-tolerable by the train driver's increasingly erratic ongoing commentary.

A delivery driver had suffered a flat tyre while crossing the line just outside of Exeter. Having inexplicably failed to charge his phone, he had decided to walk to the nearest village, only to fall into a river while attempting to get a look at a pair of swans, resulting in a hastily galvanised rescue operation which left no emergency vehicles to move the stuck delivery lorry from the line. He had apparently been pulled out of the Dart Estuary some time later, babbling about mermaids and fish that could talk.

At least, that was how it had been relayed over the train's announcement system, in such excruciating detail that the passenger sitting beside Madeline had torn pages

I

out of his book, stuffed them into his ears, and attempted to go to sleep. The notification board at Brentwell Station, warning of delays caused by a fallen tree, was something of an anti-climax.

Madeline's father, Jonas Fellow, was waiting for her at the station, which brought both joy at seeing him for the first time in so long, and regret at the absence of her mother. He saw her the moment she alighted, threw his arms open wide and pulled her into a warm bear hug. In an instant she was a little girl again, finding safety and comfort in her daddy's arms. Then she pulled away, noticed how much he had aged, and remembered just how many years had passed.

'I'm sorry I couldn't come home sooner,' she said. 'I wanted to come back for the funeral. I really did.' She sniffed, wiping away a tear. 'I'm kind of a little … angry that I wasn't told.'

Jonas looked down, giving a little shake of his head. 'I'm sorry. I wanted to tell you, but … it was what she wanted. She knew what you were doing was important to you.' He sniffed. 'I know we were divorced, but I was still fond of your mother. And the way she would never let her health put a dampener on anyone else was just her all over. She didn't want anyone to wear black at her funeral. It was all Hawaiian shirts and floral dresses. We looked ridiculous, but your mother would have loved it.'

'I still would have liked to be there. I could have ended my contract sooner.'

'I know. I'm sorry. I only did what your mother asked. And really, when you think about what she always said—that a funeral was a little bit late to be saying goodbye—it makes perfect sense. You spoke to her on video call the night before she died. She died in her sleep, Madeline. You were the last person to see her alive.'

'The last thing she said was that she loved me,' Madeline said. 'And I said, "Mum, don't be so soppy." I wish I'd told her that I loved her instead.'

Jonas put an arm around her shoulders. 'It's just words,' he said. 'She knew. Anyone can say the words, but love that's been growing over a lifetime doesn't need any. She knew you loved her.'

'Thanks for saying that.'

Jonas clapped his hands together. 'So, you're back in England. My little girl. And you've lost weight, by the look of things. I imagine it's all that running on Australian beaches. Don't worry, we'll soon sort you out. Pasties or fish'n'chips for your first meal back home?'

'How about pasties with a portion of chips, and a fish to go halves on?'

Jonas grinned. 'That's my little girl.'

There were a couple of good takeaways across the street from the station, so they picked up their order then walked to a little park nearby and sat on a bench beside the river. The sky was clear, the air crisp, with clouds building behind the hills on the far horizon threatening rain later in the evening.

'Are you sure you're all right, Dad?' Madeline said, as they started to eat. Out across the river, a couple of ducks twisted among the reeds.

Jonas nodded. 'Don't worry about me, love. It's been a little strange getting used to retirement, that's all. Your mother's death didn't help.'

'I can imagine.' She patted him on the knee. 'You're your own man, now, though, aren't you? No more business meetings or weekends at the office.'

The words probably came out a little more bitter than she intended, like a coffee with not enough milk. Jonas looked at her.

'I wasn't that bad, was I? I gave you and Eric as much of my time as I could.'

'I'm sorry, I didn't mean it like that.'

Jonas sighed. 'I know. It was always on my mind, you know, while you were growing up. Am I working too much, am I spending enough time with you and your mother? I never forgave myself for missing your netball final with that stupid client golf day.'

Madeline laughed. At the time she had been gutted not to see his face in the crowd, but by the end of the game it had felt like a relief.

'We got hammered,' she said. 'I was kind of glad you weren't there.'

Jonas gave a dismissive shrug. 'You know, your mother often felt like you went overseas because you harboured some sort of resentment towards us,' he said. 'I think that's natural that parents think their kids hate them.'

Madeline shook her head. 'Of course not. I just wanted to travel, that's all. It's been eight years, though. It might be time to settle down, at least for a bit.'

Jonas tossed a chip into the river. Immediately, half a dozen ducks came racing towards it, quacking like maniacs, water splashing up behind them.

'Well, me and Brentwell are glad to have you back,' Jonas said. 'Even if it's only temporary.'

'Probably not my little brother, though. I imagine he'll start with the whole return-of-the-golden-child thing as soon as he sees me.'

Jonas laughed. 'I think he has other things on his mind.'

'I can't believe he's getting married. My slimy little

brother is actually getting married. What's she like? Does she keep paper towels in her purse to dry his sweaty palms?'

'Don't be unkind,' Jonas said with a smile. 'She's actually very nice, is Amy. She's a little bit OCD, though. He told me she organised his sock drawer, lining them all up by their order in the colour spectrum, with the toe bits all pointing inwards. He said it makes his eyes go funny to look at it.'

'Good on her for taking him off the streets,' Madeline said. 'I imagine there were street parties among the single women of Brentwell when they found out.'

'Don't be horrible,' Jonas said. 'They look very happy together. So, let's talk about you. How long are you planning to stay? Are you going to get a job now you're back? Of course, you're welcome to your old room at mine for as long as you like.'

'Thanks, Dad. I don't know, though. I really just came to pay my respects to Mum. I'll probably get a job for a bit, but I'm not sure how long I'll stay. I've been away a long time, but most of the people I knew before I left are still here. It'll be weird seeing them again. I don't know if I'll fit in anymore.'

'Well, let's take it a day at a time.' Jonas put his empty chips carton into the plastic bag the shop had given them. 'Wow, that filled a hole. Are you ready? Let's get you home.'

2

———

GHOSTS

REDFIELD, their suburb of Brentwell, to the southwest of the town centre, looked almost spookily like Madeline remembered it. Mr. Davies at Number 14 still had his purple Robin Reliant, and the broken hinge on the hanging sign outside the Redfield Tavern still hadn't been fixed, even though Matt, the landlord, had been promising to get it done since Madeline had been old enough to buy a drink. One of the trees along Redfield Canal, which joined up with Willow River, had been replaced by a sycamore sapling, but the other nine in the row on the embankment on the tavern's side still stood as they always had.

'A lorry slipped on ice last winter and ran into it,' Jonas told her by way of explanation as she craned her neck out of the car's side window to look. 'It was all right, but one of the roots on the road side got disturbed, and kids kept tripping on it. A shame, really.'

'I imagine Amy struggles with it.'

'She closes her eyes when they drive past, Eric told me,'

Jonas said. 'By the way, are you planning to catch up with any of your old friends while you're home?'

'I'm not sure.'

They pulled into Lock Keepers Lane and came to a stop outside Jonas's quiet suburb house. 'I saw Lucinda the other day in Tesco,' Jonas said. 'She had a newborn with her.' He grinned. 'I assume it was hers.'

'I saw she was pregnant last time I stalked her on Facebook,' Madeline said with a smile. 'I don't know. We haven't really kept in touch.'

'Come on, you have loads in common. She sells holidays. You go on them.'

'It was a working holiday,' Madeline said. 'As in, I only get to bum around pools on weekends. It's not quite the same, though, is it? I mean, I've been out of the country a while.'

'She's put on weight too,' Jonas said. 'I doubt you'll be running any cross-country races together like you used to.'

'That'll be having kids for you,' Madeline said.

'You know, I wouldn't be disappointed if you found out,' Jonas said. 'I'm not holding out on Amy putting up with Eric long enough to provide me with some grandchildren I can hammer at chess and Connect 4.'

'Don't give up, Dad.'

'Not for a couple more years. Talking of children, are you going to see Rory while you're home?'

'Dad … are you suggesting that Rory is a child, or that he's the closest person I've so far come to having a child with?'

Jonas, having finished reversing up the drive, leaving the car pointed like an arrow down at the kerb, switched off the engine and shrugged.

'Ah … maybe both?'

'He wasn't that bad, Dad. We were just at different

stages of our lives.'

'You mean that you wanted to be an adult while he wanted to continue getting hammered and attempting to jump across the canal on a Friday night? If he'd got a couple of feet closer to the far edge, it might have knocked some sense into him.'

'You remember that time he broke his ankle on a submerged shopping trolley? He was convinced it was you who put it in there.'

Dad opened the side door. 'Not guilty. Wish I was.'

They got out of the car. Evening was coming on, and a gentle breeze was shaking the trees and shrubs in the front gardens along Lock Keepers Lane. Madeline glanced up at the sky, already streaked with purples and oranges as the sun slowly sank towards the west. She'd get a couple of nice weeks, for sure, to wander around Brentwell, perhaps take a stroll through Sycamore Park like she used to, maybe see if the Oak Leaf Café was still there and get a maple latte, just for old time's sake. Then the evenings would draw in, the leaves would fall, and it would be cold and gloomy for the next six months.

She had never liked autumn. It was thRoryguard for winter, a little teaser for the horrid days to come. Summer was good for a visit, but Madeline was usually back on a plane and safely stowed away overseas somewhere by now. It was strange to be coming back at the exact time she normally went away.

'I'm taking your silence as an "I don't want to talk about it slash yes. I mean, I know your mother didn't like him, so by default I should have thought he was the best thing since the four-slice toaster, but it was hard not to agree.'

Madeline sighed. 'I'm not planning to contact him,' she said. 'Is he even still around? We don't exactly keep in touch. When I turned down the thrilling opportunity to live in a caravan with him on his parents' front lawn in order to go and work overseas, it didn't go down well.'

In fact, Rory had thrown a tantrum, quite literally throwing his toys out of his pram—although in this case it was his cups and bowls out of his caravan—and then gone up to the Tavern to get drunk, before heading down to the canal for another attempt to jump across the width of its green, murky waters.

She was yet to know whether he had made it or not, but during the last eight years, through the course of which she had—among other things—worked as a private English teacher for an Indonesian diplomat, washed dishes in a Japanese ski resort, spent some time as an English-speaking tour guide at Anchor Wat, picked durian on a farm in Vietnam, and most recently worked as an au pair, nannying two delightful infant daughters of an Australian politician—Rory and his issues had been a long way from her mind.

'That's good,' Jonas said. 'I mean, he might have changed his spots, but a leopard can't change its internal organs, can it?'

'Huh? What on earth are you talking about?'

Jonas just gave an uncomfortable shrug. 'You'll see. Well, hopefully you won't. Anyway, let's get you inside. Are you hungry? Because I can order a pizza or something if you are.'

'We only had dinner half an hour ago.'

Jonas shrugged. 'Well, got to keep your strength up, haven't you? Who knows what surprises might be waiting for you now you're home.'

'Not too many, I hope.'

Jonas just gave her another pained look, but this time he said nothing.

3

FAMILY REUNION

DAD WANTED to come with her up to the churchyard, but having missed out on the funeral, Madeline preferred to say a private goodbye to her mother.

All that was left of Elizabeth Claire Tremaine—known for most of her life as Beth Fellow—was a granite plaque embedded into a concrete wall at the back of Redfield church, in the shadows beneath a towering sycamore tree. Jonas and Eric had chosen a nice spot for the woman who had brought Madeline into the world and then spent the next thirty-two years hassling her through it. Childhood had never been easy, but neither had it been an unmitigated disaster. While her brother Eric, younger by four years, had always been her mother's favourite, and the perennial baby of the family, a situation which had led him to grow up into a slimy wannabe heartbreaker whose greatest asset was the ability to drive flies away whenever he came too close, her father had always been more measured about his love for his children. Madeline suspected, although Jonas would never admit it, that due to the virtue of her mother's obvious slant towards Eric's side that she might just edge ahead on his. Mum had never missed an occasion to shower Eric with affection, but if Madeline came home with a good school report or won a trophy in cross-country running, Mum had been quick enough to get in the cakes or insist they went out to celebrate. Madeline didn't miss her like she would miss her father when he died, but she did still miss her. And that was enough.

'Nice flowers, Mum,' she said, pushing a bunch of foxgloves aside to slide in the carnations she had bought from the Tesco Metro up on the high street. She suspected the foxgloves were her brother's work; they looked sponged from a park flowerbed. 'I'm sorry I couldn't be there for your funeral. But, you know, that was technically your fault for insisting that no one tell me. I would have come back, you know. You weren't that much of a dragon, and I did always feel guilty that I left Eric to care for you all these years.'

She felt guilty, yes, but Eric had volunteered and been happy about it. Dad had done his bit to help, too, even though they had been divorced five years before her health started to fail. Eric had consumed himself with caring for Mum, moving her into his little two-bed semi a mile north of Brentwell Primary School where he worked. In truth, while it pained her to admit it, at twenty-eight and about to get married he was probably doing far better financially than she was: after all, the kind of short-term overseas jobs she lived for didn't pay particularly well, and what money she did manage to save generally got burned up the next time she had a couple of weeks off for free travelling. Having found herself back in England in September, she was in the unenviable position of actually needing to get a job and earn some money before she could afford to go back overseas. There were always teaching jobs, but nowhere paid well these days, and there were startup costs everywhere. She had her eye on South America this time, planning to leave late autumn or early winter, to get out there before Christmas. She had already invited Dad to visit wherever she was, although Eric and his soon-to-be-wife had also invited him, meaning an inevitable tug-of-war would soon start. Of course, none of that would be a factor if she didn't start earning some money.

Tesco was hiring, and she'd seen a sign up in the window of the local fish'n'chips shop. Evans Carpets up on Fore Street was looking for a delivery driver, but she needed to update her license details. She'd planned to do a bit of English teaching, but it seemed that Brexit had caused the only local community classes to shut down.

What to do? She wandered up to the Job Centre, but even here in Brentwell there were a handful of scary benefits types hanging around outside, so even though they dressed a lot nicer than they did in other cities and there wasn't a can of Special Brew to be seen, she was too nervous to go inside. Instead, she wandered up the high street for a while, stopping for coffee in a boutique café where the owner stared at her for so long Madeline began to wonder if she had a spot on her forehead, then doing some window shopping, picking up a couple of interesting bits and bobs in one of the charity shops, and an Eagles CD for Dad.

By the time she got back to Dad's it was half past five. To her surprise, a posh BMW was parked in the driveway.

Voices drifted out from the living room as she came in the front door. She took off her shoes and hung her jacket on a hook. She recognised Dad's voice, and when a second male voice rose, she felt an urge to put her shoes back on and make a run for the nearest pub.

Just get it over with.

'Hello,' she said, pushing open the living room door. 'I'm back.'

Her brother, Eric—who had insisted on Rick since secondary school as though that would somehow make him less of a dweeb—stood by the sideboard behind the sofa, holding a bottle of Dad's whisky in his hands. To the best of Madeline's knowledge, he had only drunk it once, when he was seventeen, and had been sick all over the kitchen table.

Dad was sitting at the dinner table by the wall, holding a cup of coffee. And on the sofa in front of Rick was a young woman. She was shorter and rounder than Madeline had expected, but a bob of hair and spectacles made her look sweet. She was tugging at the nearest armrest cover as though trying to realign it.

'Ah, look, the wanderer returns,' Rick said. 'Nice to see you again, Madster.'

Madeline winced. It was starting already. Like an old car cranking back into life, the bickering that had defined them from childhood through young adulthood was about to begin. She opened her mouth to snap at him to call her Madeline, knowing that the words would be some kind of magic spell which would cause him to spend the rest of the evening calling her Madster or Madman, or Maddiloops, or Madelinifer, or one of a dozen other made up versions of her actual name. Then, with the words still on her tongue, she closed her mouth again, and smiled.

'Hi, Rick. How are you? And this must be Amy?'

Rick was still staring at her, a look of disappointment in his eyes at her failure to rise to his challenge. Amy snapped up off of the sofa, brushed herself down— spending an overly long time adjusting the cuff of the shirt she wore—then gave a genial smile.

'Hello, my name is Amy Clairmont,' she said. 'You must be Madeline? Rick's sister? It's lovely to meet you.'

She stuck out a hand. Madeline came forwards and gave it a little shake.

'And you,' she said, immediately feeling sorry for this poor girl who had a lifetime of living with her brother ahead of her. But perhaps one man's trash was another's gold, and all that.

'I do hope we can be friends,' Amy said, shaking Madeline's hand a little too hard.

'Sure,' Madeline said. 'I'd like that.'

'I thought it would be nice for Rick and Amy to come over for dinner,' Jonas said. Then, with a grin, added, 'I've ordered some Indian from the takeaway on Fore Street.'

'Sounds great.'

'So, Father, this is the dram you ordered in from Japan?' Rick said, turning the bottle of whisky around. 'I can tell just from the feel of the bottle that it's exotic.'

'That's right,' Jonas said, catching Madeline's look and giving her a smile. 'Via the shop on the corner.'

Amy was still standing up, like a soldier waiting for orders. Madeline didn't feel appropriate telling a woman she'd only just met to sit down, so in an attempt to change the topic, she wandered to the window, peered out at the BMW, then said to Rick, 'Nice wheels. Is that yours or Amy's?'

Rick put the bottle of whisky back in Jonas's drink's cabinet and turned to face Madeline, a smug grin on his face.

'Mine,' he said. 'Of course. With the promotion I got a credit deal up at Jake's Motors.'

'So it's not actually yours?'

'It's a new scheme,' Rick said, adopting the condescending tone he'd been using with her since he'd first climbed out of his cradle. It wasn't a new scheme at all, but it was easier to humour him than get into an argument. 'Plus, I have a few more points in the bank with the promotion.'

She could see in his eyes how desperate he was for her to ask about this promotion. Jonas's eyes were flicking back and forth between them with a grin on his face that suggested he was delighted to have his children back together, while Amy had finally sat back down and was now fiddling with the tassels along the bottom of the sofa cushions, trying to straighten them.

'It's quite a jump from a Ford Fiesta to a BMW,' Madeline said.

Rick shrugged. 'A car's a car at the end of the day,' he said. 'I mean, automatic mirror tilting, parked car ventilation, home pathway lighting functions … they're all just bells and whistles, aren't they? I have to admit, there was probably a little vanity involved with the upgrade, but they really had to push it on me. I was happy enough with the last old thing, but with the promotion comes a certain expectation, you know? Such is this materialistic world we live in. I mean, in our shallow, shallow world, it's the car that defines the man, isn't it?'

It was best just to get it out of the way. 'So, you got promoted, did you? Are there many promotions available for primary school teachers?'

Rick's smile could have made birds fall from the sky. 'Only to acting head,' he said.

'Acting head,' Amy echoed her voice filled with pride.

'Quite the achievement at your age,' Jonas said, sipping his coffee. 'A bit of experience in the role now and it might be yours permanently one day.'

'I see the emphasis is on "acting"?' Madeline said, trying so hard not to sound patronising.

Rick shrugged. 'It's admittedly short term,' he said. 'Mr. Downton, our current figurehead, got himself hooked up with the broad who owns the café up in Sycamore Park. He's taking a sabbatical so they can go off travelling in India for three months.'

'The broad?'

'Her name's Angela,' Amy said. 'I think they're in love.'

'Which means he might not come back,' Rick said. 'Or you know, there's malaria. And tigers. So I think it's best if I treated this position as though it could become permanent.'

'How lucky for your staff to have you as a leader,' Madeline said.

'Quite, quite.'

Amy actually gave a little clap. 'He's going to be great. Everyone likes him.'

The world really had turned, unless Amy lived in some kind of alternate reality. Madeline turned to her and said, 'It'll be nice showing up in a Bimmer every day, won't it?'

Before Amy could answer, Rick said, 'Oh, no, Amy will still be going to work in her Golf. It wouldn't do for the children to know that two of the staff are involved with each other.'

'It wouldn't do,' Amy said, sounding disappointed.

Madeline was just preparing another dig, when Jonas clapped his hands together. 'Right, let's get the food out, shall we?'

That she managed to avoid having a full-blown argument with Rick over the next two hours either proved they were both maturing, or that she had finally learned how to bite her tongue where her brother was concerned. Still, when

Rick announced that he and Amy ought to leave because he began training for his promotion in the morning, Madeline wasn't sad to see him go. He had spent all evening ribbing her about being currently unemployed, suggesting all manner of alternative short-term jobs from "one of those grubbers outside the train station trying to sign you up for a charity" to "that guy who walks behind the rubbish lorry picking up all the bits that fall out". With Dad's eyes warning her to keep on her best behaviour, she had refused to let him rile her, even when he'd suggested that in his new position he might be able to wrangle her a part time janitorial position at Brentwell Secondary.

Throughout, Amy watched Rick with utter adulation, hanging off every word when she wasn't adjusting the straightness of the placemats and cutlery. By the time they left, Madeline—who had drunk a little more wine than either Amy or Jonas, while Rick, who was driving, had maintained that condescending look that sober people loved to use when in the company of tipsy people—was starting to feel a little pining for a taste of true love. Having had her youthful optimism ruined by Rory, she had gone out into the world hoping to find it, but despite a couple of short-term relationships, the real thing had managed to elude her.

'Right, I'm off to bed,' Jonas announced, shortly after Rick and Amy had left.

'I'm just going to watch a bit of TV,' Madeline told him.

He gave her a kiss on the cheek. 'I'm very proud of you,' he said. 'I've never known you to have such powers of restraint. My little girl really has grown up.'

'I'm unemployed, Dad,' she said.

Jonas laughed. 'So am I. You don't hear me complaining, do you?'

'You're retired. That's different.'

'You might be unemployed right now, but you've already done things in your life that most people can only dream about. Remember that when you next go looking for work. Don't sell yourself short. Bits of paper with letters and numbers on them are worth nothing. Experience … that's priceless. Set your bar a little higher.'

Madeline felt a sudden burning love for her father. She pulled him into a tight hug.

'Why are you so wise?'

Jonas shrugged. 'I'm a dad. That's my real job.'

4

THE SECRETARY PROBLEM

THE NEXT DAY, Madeline headed out early with a more determined attitude. She went to the Job Centre first to sign on, plucking up the courage to go inside, but most of the jobs they had available involved sitting at desks and pressing buttons. Before going overseas, Madeline had spent a year as a temp doing insurance claims for a delivery company, and it wasn't something she was keen to repeat. She was referred to one part time job working at a wildlife centre in Birch Valley, but it was a thirty-minute train ride each way, and with a half-hour walk from Dad's to the station, she'd spend almost as much time commuting as she would working.

She declined to put in an application, but planned to return the following day for another search.

Having spent most of the morning in the job centre, she decided to get some lunchor lunch. She headed up to Brentwell's main shopping area, but her old favourite sandwich shop had closed down, replaced by an estate agent. She didn't fancy anything out of a bakery, and the only new restaurant was far too expensive for her liking.

She didn't want to sit in a pub, so, running out of options, she figured she might as well head back to Dad's.

She'd made a wide circuit of the town in her failed search for something decent to eat, and the quickest way back to Lock Keepers Lane was to cut through Sycamore Park, down by Brentwell Theatre. She had spent a lot of time in Sycamore Park during her teenage years, but not much since. Rory had liked to hang out there sometimes, and she had so far purposely avoided it through a wariness that it might stir up unwanted memories.

As the park's northern entrance appeared up ahead, with the back of the Brentwell Public Library off to one side, she recognised the little building just past the gate, a handful of tables arranged outside, and a sudden wild thought came to mind.

Madeline had always found it easier to talk to people from foreign countries, particularly if it was in a pigeon version of their own language. It was like the language barrier created a screen that absorbed any potential awkwardness or embarrassment.

When it came to speaking to someone who understood every word, however, it was a whole different matter. Suddenly the words tumbled over themselves, refusing to cooperate.

With all this in mind, Madeline approached the door to the Oak Leaf Café with a lump of trepidation in her throat. Even before she reached the quaint wooden door with twisting roses growing out of two large pots on either side making a pretty green and red arch, she had lost the ability to speak. She stood there dumbly, looking at the latticed windows, their frames tainted with just enough age to be vintage rather than decrepit. She stared through the reflections of the giant sycamore trees in this corner of the park at the wood-paneled interior, at the tables designed for couples and small families, pots of salt and pepper, handwritten menus in ornate wire-framed holders. She saw the sign hanging in the window advertising for a temporary manager, but even as she continued to stare at it, her nerves got the better of her, and she was about to turn and flee when the door suddenly opened and a spritely middle-aged woman in an apron appeared. Long brown hair flecked with grey was tied back in a ponytail that swung over her shoulder. She pushed spectacles up her nose and smiled a youthful smile.

'Hello, dear. You have the honour of being today's first customer. That means you get a free slice of maple and pecan pie with whatever else you order. It's a bit chilly, so why don't you sit inside? Menu's on the table.' As Madeline continued to stare at her, the woman tilted her head. 'Wow, are those dreadlocks? How cool. May I touch them?'

At mention of her hair, something sparked Madeline back into life. 'Ah, no, they're just plaits that have been that way for a very long time. Someone in Australia did them for me, and showed me a way to extend them without having to untie them. You have to get the ends and fold them back in up at the top, like this.' She started to demonstrate, then stopped. 'Ah, you probably don't want to know.'

'I'm fascinated. At my age my next haircut will probably be my last, so I want to get some mileage out of it first. You look like a bit of a hair person. Why don't you come in and give me some tips?' She glanced up at the sky and frowned. 'Looks like it's going to rain. Your only other food options are Pete's van down on the south side, but he's probably gone home, or that hideous fast-food place up around the corner. I'll trade you lunch for some beauty tips.'

'I don't know any beauty tips—'

'Oh, you do.' The woman grinned. 'Look at you. I can see the world in you, and that's more beautiful than anything else.'

Madeline choked back a sudden, unexpected sob. 'Oh.'

'Dear, what's wrong? Come inside and tell Angela your problems over something filled with sugar and maple syrup.'

Two and a half hours and several cups of sugary coffee later, Madeline was leaning over a window table, telling Angela in intricate detail about a bus journey down through the hills of Vietnam.

'And we were like, this far from the edge of this ravine,' she said, hands held close together. 'It was like a computer game. It's this dirt road, and we're just hacking it round these corners, swinging out over the sides, and no one seemed remotely concerned. And then we suddenly come to a stop in the middle of nowhere. The driver just gets out and wanders into this wooden shack, so one by one we all get off. And I swear, all they had inside this shed place was a big freezer filled with ice-cream.'

Angela gave a fluttery laugh. 'Oh, that sounds so exciting. I'm going to have to get Greg to take me there after we're done with India. He wants to go up to Norway and see the fjords. I think he's only doing the hippy trail to humour me. He just wants to spend three months buying jackets and sunglasses. Men, aren't they so dull?'

'I don't currently have one. That's one of the tragedies of moving from country to country.'

'Ah, love them and leave them. That's the way you want to do it when you're young. Play the field and all that. You've heard of the secretary problem, haven't you?'

'Ah, no.'

'It's a statistical theory. It used to be called the marriage problem, but then people got a little gas in their bellies about that. Although perhaps these days it should be the P.A. problem, ho hum.' Before Madeline could reply, Angela held up a hand. 'You're interviewing for a job, and you have to reject or select based on each person's ability, without knowing the ability of the rest. You only get one chance, and you can't go back.'

'Right....'

'So, the way the formula works, is that you should reject the first thirty-seven percent, regardless of how impressive they are, then you should hire the very next person you interview who is better than anyone in the first thirty-seven percent.'

'So what that means is—'

'Let's say you're looking for someone to marry, and you're willing to ... let's say, *investigate* a hundred people in total.'

'Oh, my—'

'Well, dump the first thirty-seven, regardless. Then pick the first one after that, who's better than the first lot. And that person will be the perfect person to marry. It's a proven theory.'

'I'm not quite sure I'm there yet.'

'Oh, if you're a little shy, you can divide your totals a little, perhaps date three people and give the fourth just a peck on the cheek. But, as someone a little higher up the age tree than you, I'd suggest you play the field a little longer. Enjoy yourself.'

'Right.' Madeline finished the last of her latte and made to stand up. 'It's been so lovely to talk to you, Angela, but I'm staying with my dad and he's going to start wondering where I am. I haven't sorted a phone out yet, so I'd better get back.'

Angela rubbed her hands together. 'So, I'll see you tomorrow?'

'Tomorrow?'

'For your training. I can't leave my café in the hands of someone untrained, can I?'

'Oh, about the—'

Angela tilted her head and smiled. 'That's why you came, isn't it? To apply for the job? You were staring at the advertisement in the window so hard I thought you were trying to move it with your eyes.'

'Yes, that's right, I did. I just need something to tie me over for a while. But don't you have to interview other candidates? Uh, like thirty-seven or so?'

Angela shook her head. 'Nope, you'll do. See you tomorrow.'

5

TRAINING

MADELINE HAD MADE countless cups of coffee for herself at home over the years, even some more exotic variations involving added ingredients and toppings, but when required to make one for a total stranger, it suddenly became the hardest thing in the world.

'So, how much milk should I put in?'

'Enough to make it taste good.'

'How much is that?'

'Use your judgement, dear. And failing that, use one of the customers as a test bunny. But never the old ladies. They're the connoisseurs. Get it wrong, and you'll be slandered in Women's Institute meetings all over Brentwell. With the old ladies, always ask. Makes them feel important. If you're looking for a tester, pick an office type, particularly one with sweat under the arms.'

'That's gross.'

Angela grinned. 'It means he's tired. You could stir a spoonful of caffeine into a glass of water and he'd gratefully drink it, but if you prepare him something good, you'll see his eyes light up. It's like you've just plugged them into the mains.'

'Okay, guys with sweat under the arms.'

'Or mothers with children. Always add an extra half a spoonful of sugar. They usually need the energy.'

'Right, got it.'

'Okay, next thing. We need to get those swirly patterns in the cream down.'

'How do you do those?'

'Oh, it's easy. Takes a bit of practice. The customers love it, though. Especially if you come up with a few unique designs. Mine especially like the squirrel. If you screw it up and it turns out just a splodge, put a dot of chocolate powder at one end and tell them it's a hedgehog.' Angela tapped her nose with a finger. 'Insider secret.'

'I never realised so much thought went into running a coffee shop.'

Angela's smile dropped. 'The problem is, that for most these days, it doesn't. All these chain places popping up everywhere, relying on famous brand names to sell their rubbish generic coffee, they're the scourge of our existence. Us independents can't compete with their prices or their product range, or even their posh, imported stools and chairs. What we have to offer our customers is a personal touch. People want to feel human.'

'That's sad. I mean, about the chain places.'

Angela smiled again. 'The revolution has begun, don't you worry. Thanks to that big messy thing on every computer and phone in the land, the little people are rising up to retake the world from the corporates. There are more boutique coffee shops, specialist retailers, and independent producers than ever before. But it's taking time, because it went really far down before it started to come back up. I remember when Brentwell's centre was a hive of shoppers every Saturday morning, going from shop to shop. Then they built two massive supermarkets, one at each end of town, and the centre was gutted. For years, all you could see were charity shops and estate agents. Things are changing now, but we're only at the beginning of the revolution.'

'I imagine it's pretty stressful being a revolutionary,' Madeline said.

Angela thumped a fist into her palm. 'And that's why we need more coffee,' she said. 'More, more, more!' She gave a little shake of her head and grinned. Then, at a tinkle of the bell over the door, her eyes widened. 'Ah ha. Customers. Are you ready?'

'No.'

'Be brave. It's just coffee.'

In the afternoon, they started on the pies. Angela had a couple of dozen recipes for various seasonal specialities, most scrawled on crumpled pieces of paper that to Madeline were barely legible.

'So long as you master the basics,' Angela said. 'That's all that counts. The amount of seasoning, the length of time to bake it, the optimum time to let it stand before serving … the rest is a world of possibilities.' She spread her arms as though to emphasise her point. 'The people who come here aren't looking for something generic that tastes the same day in, day out. Remind me what they're looking for?'

'The personal touch.'

Angela clicked her fingers. 'Ta da! Give them the personal touch, a smile, and a bit of conversation if they need it, and they'll be back again. I guarantee it. Don't overdo it, though. Some people come for company, some people are good on their own. You'll learn to spot them. If they keep glancing up, fidgeting, shifting their chair around, they're waiting for something, usually a bit of attention. Wander over and have a word. If they turn their chair to the window and pull out a book or—god forbid—a smartphone, leave them to it. They're happy in their solitude or their devices.'

'It must take years to figure out all this.'

'Less time than you'd think. You just need to find a tuning that connects you to other people. Then, voila! You have a vibrant and successful café full of happy, returning customers.' Angela lifted a finger. 'But remember, while they're customers, they're still just people. Sure, you'll get a few weirdos—that's inevitable—but if you find someone you like, or—' She narrowed her eyes and smiled, '—even someone you *love*, slide right in there.' Angela made a grand sweeping gesture with her hand, like an ice-skater preparing to pirouette.

'I'll try to remember that.'

Angela smiled. 'You'll do great.'

For the next three days, Angela took Madeline through all the main points for running a café.

'Right, this list here, these are the suppliers. Oak Leaf Café is vegetarian, but we're not vegan—there's a big difference. Martin Donbury, he supplies all our dairy products. Then there's Reg—aren't all greengrocers called Reg, ha?—who supplies the vegetables. Kaitin Compre—she's French, I believe—she's our coffee supplier. And down the list we go. These are all people I've worked with for years, so keep them sweet. Some deliver weekly, others every other day. Some once a month. It's all there in the ledger. And if you need to adjust anything, just give them a call.'

'Got it.'

'Right, the boring stuff. This book is our accounts. Gross sales minus expenses equals our profit. That number needs to stay above that number. That's pretty much it.'

'Seems self-explanatory.'

'It is. And the last thing, when you go home, lights off, alarm on. That's about it. We're not likely to be broken into. The glorious council budgeted for us to have a night warden from this year. His name's Daniel. He's very nice. You'll meet him in the early mornings as he often comes in for coffee before going home. Give him a free piece of cake if you have any left over. Can't be a terribly rewarding job looking after an empty park at night.'

'I will.'

'Right.' Angela looked up, rubbing her hands together. 'So, I think we're all set. Any questions, you can't ask, because I'll likely be off the grid, rejecting civilisation and all that. I'll be home in the new year unless I get assimilated into some remote hill tribe, so the café's all yours until then. I don't like to discuss money, because it's so boring, but as the tyrannical landlord you can save me twenty-percent. All the rest—minus utilities and supplier costs, of course—is yours. Happy caféing.'

Madeline couldn't help but smile. 'I can't thank you enough for this opportunity. When do you want me to start?'

Angela grinned. 'Tomorrow morning will be fine. My dear beau Greg—he of the tight wallet—booked us a nice redeye. We take off at midnight.'

'*Tonight?*'

'Yep. A taxi's coming in half an hour.' Angela spread

her arms. 'Woah, I'd better get packing! Was there anything else?'

Madeline's heart was fluttering with nerves. 'Uh, I don't think so....'

'Great!' Angela patted her on the arm. 'Good luck!'

6

———

UNDER NEW MANAGEMENT

IT WAS a fine September morning when Madeline set out for her first day as the acting manager of Sycamore Park's Oak Leaf Café. Jonas gave her a big send off by cooking her an enormous English breakfast, doubling up both the sausages and the bacon, in order to 'counteract all that lettuce you've got to eat at work', although it amused him when she reminded him that both coffee and sugar—two of the main staples of any good café—were both plants.

Sycamore Park looked delightful with the sun gleaming through leaves that were yet to start changing colour, although Madeline found herself darkly pleased that the tree beneath which she and Rory had shared their first kiss had been cut down, reduced to a flat stump with a couple of small saplings growing nearby. A group of ducks quacked amicably at each other as they poked in the reeds around the fishpond. A pair of old people power-walking with silver weights gripped tightly in their hands and unnecessary luminous headbands keeping the sweat out of their eyes gave her a stoic 'good morning', while a young woman walking a little dog smiled as she passed.

Set among a stand of trees to the side of the town library, the Oak Leaf Café lingered like a waiting lover, embroiled with endless possibilities. Originally a simple two-storey redbrick, the nearby trees and an abundance of potted plants and trellised roses gave it a secretive, fairytale look. The tables standing outside, currently with umbrellas closed and chairs upturned, offered endless adventures and stories yet to be told. Madeline was practically bouncing as she reached it, fumbling in her pocket for the key.

A few minutes later, she was still trying to get the old key to fit into a lock that on closer inspection really needed an oiling, when a cheery voice called out, 'Hey there! Top of the morning, to you. Are you open for a fine cup of coffee yet?'

She turned to see a middle-aged, balding man in an apron standing nearby. He duffed an imaginary hat and gave a half-bow.

'Um, hello.'

'Over-applied the moisturiser this morning, have you, Angela? Or did you dig up a time machine in your garden yesterday?'

'Ah, I'm not Angela,' Madeline said, stating what she hoped was obvious. 'My name is Madeline Fellow. I'm going to be running this place for a while in Angela's absence.'

The man's eyes widened. 'Of course, that's right. I remember her saying. Well, it's nice to meet you. I'm Pete Markham, your competition. On that shabby burger van down yonder. Don't worry, my filthy old dregs aren't a patch on your smorgasbord of caffeine-infused delights, but there's always that demographic which likes their coffee like their clothes: cheap, and short-lived.'

Madeline stared. 'Pete? Pete Markham? Wow, you

probably don't remember me. Last time I saw you, you had … ah, hair.'

Pete grinned. 'Still a few strands left, gamely holding on.'

'My friends and I used to come down here for burgers after a night out back in the day.'

'Back when I did the late shift? Long passed that, I'm afraid. Need my beauty sleep. More and more of it as the years pass. Aren't you that girl who threw up over my sign that one time?'

Madeline smiled. 'Oh, god, I remember that. But no, it wasn't me. That was Emily, one of my school friends. Wow, I wonder what happened to her?'

'Hopefully she's passed the puking-on-burger-vans stage by now.'

'Most of us grow out of it,' Madeline said. 'How can I help you, Pete?'

'Angela always used to fix me up a decent brew of a morning,' Pete said. Then, grinning, he added, 'I don't mind selling my stuff, but I don't want to drink it.'

'No worries, give me a minute to get this door open.'

'You have to lift it slightly as you twist it,' Pete said. 'One of the hinges is slightly loose. Both me and Tom—the park's caretaker—have been on at her for years to fix it, but she likes her quirks, does Angela.'

Taking his advice, Madeline pulled the door upwards slightly, and the key turned without hesitation.

'Thanks!'

'No worries. You look like you might be busy. Do you want me to come back later?'

'No, it's okay. I've got to get used to it.'

'I'll sort these tables out for you.'

'Thanks, Pete. That's kind of you.'

As Madeline went inside, Pete began taking the chairs

down from the tabletops and putting up the umbrellas. Madeline went to turn on the lights, the realised she had no idea where the switches were. Angela had definitely told her, but she had probably also mentioned about the door.

'Ah, Pete?' Madeline called out through the doorway. 'I don't suppose you know where the light switches are?'

'Behind the hedgehog painting, just inside the door,' Pete called.

'Ah, got it.'

With a click, the café's gloomy interior filled with warm light. Madeline gave a contented sigh. Angela had known a thing or two about interior design. Intricate wire pots hung from the wall, currently filled with dried flowers. Each table was set into its own little nook, with either a window view or a view of the café's interior, leaving no one to have to face the wall. There were a dozen tables, half of them for two people, half for four, but the way the café was laid out made it feel much smaller, like every table was the focus, every potential customer important.

The serving counter took up one wall, glass display boxes in front of a preparation worktop, with five stools along the outer side for solo customers. There was a low shelf in front of the display boxes for these customers to put their drinks on while they gazed at the cakes in the display boxes. Each position was marked with a bowl of polished stones, a tea cup filled with dried flowers, and a handwritten menu glued to dark brown card and propped up in a holder made out of a hand-length piece of tree branch sliced in half and with a groove cut into the curved top. The menu advertised a multitude of coffees and various meals, only a few of which Angela had taught Madeline how to prepare.

She found the coffee machine and switched it on. Angela had a variety of devices, depending on what was ordered. On the shelves over the machine were several expensive coffee grinders lined up like ornaments.

She made Pete a coffee as well as one for herself and took them both outside. Pete had finished setting the tables and was sitting down at one, hands behind his head, whistling to himself.

'Thank you, dear,' Pete said, sitting up as she set the coffee down.

'Welcome,' Madeline said with a smile. 'You're my first customer.'

'I'm honoured. Fine day like this, you might get a few more. Rumour has it, there's a bus load of grandmas coming down for a matinee show over at the theatre there. I hope you've got your pies cooked.'

'Oh, really? I'm afraid I'm not really sure what I'm doing. I sort of threw my name into the hat, but now I've got the job, I'm kind of scared I'll mess everything up. Angela probably should have picked someone more capable.'

Pete chuckled. 'She's a good judge of character, is Angela. If she hired you, then she knows you'll do a good job. Sometimes it takes a bit of practice, but you'll get there. My daughter Lily came home this time last year in a right pickle. She'd just quit her city job, and she was wandering around like a headless chicken. My brother gave her a job in his guesthouse, and fast forward a year, she's running the place. He's off taking his first holiday in twenty years. You know what the most important thing is?'

'What?'

'To do it with heart. Put your heart in there, and you can't go wrong.' Pete leaned forwards, reached into his pocket, and pulled out his wallet.

Madeline put up a hand. 'It's all right, it's on the house. You've helped me out too much already.'

Pete shook his head. 'I appreciate the gesture. In that case, let me give you a pound for your tip jar, start you off in the right way. But I also wanted to give you this.'

He handed her a business card. Madeline looked down and read, Peter Markham, Mural Artist. On the back was his address and phone number.

'You're an artist?'

Pete grinned. 'Not just a cheeky burger van owner. That patio over by the trees there, that was my design.'

'Really? That's amazing.'

'I just wanted to say, if you have any trouble, give me a call. If I can't help, I'll know someone who can.'

'Thanks, Pete. I really appreciate it.'

'No worries. And talking of helpers, there's one. Hey, Dan!'

An old man in a duffel coat was leading a black Labrador on a lead down the path that led towards the theatre. He lifted his head at Pete's shout and tugged the dog's lead.

'Hello there,' he said, limping over. 'A good morning to you, Pete. I see you're getting into the good stuff.'

'Got a big vat of me own dregs on the brew down in thRory,' Pete said. 'Why don't you pull up a seat? This young lady here is Madeline Fellow. She's running the café while Angela's off on her travels.'

'Oh, aye.' The man peered at Madeline. He really was quite a sight. His hair and beard were a wiry mess of grey and white, the hair just about contained by a flat cap. A couple of twigs had got caught in his beard, although he either hadn't noticed or didn't care. The most striking feature, though, was a green glass bead where his left eye had been. Looking him directly in the face was quite a challenge; the bead blinked and moved like a regular eye, revealing swirling, hypnotic patterns.

'Name's Daniel Rathbone,' the old man said. 'Me's the park nightwatchman.'

'Oh, you're the Daniel that Angela mentioned.'

'That'll be me.'

'Let me get you a coffee.'

'Honoured.'

She hurried inside, prepared a quick cup and brought it back out. Then, remembering the dog, she hurried back inside, searching for something she could use as a water bowl. The only thing she could see was a plastic salad dish, so she quickly filled it from the tap and took it back outside. Halfway to the table, she caught her foot on a corner of paving and stumbled, splashing half the water over the table.

'So sorry!'

Pete and Dan laughed. 'Relax,' Pete said.

'Lass, it looks like you've been up all night, not me,' Dan said as Madeline gathered herself and put what was left of the water down for the dog to drink. 'Sit back down and take it easy. Take over Milady, here.'

'Milady?'

''Tis my fine girl's name,' Dan said. 'Although you'd better watch out if you're doing something inappropriate down here of an evening. A right terror, she is.'

'How long have you been the nightwatchman?' Madeline asked.

Daniel shrugged. 'Just from this April. Council suddenly seems to like this old place after ignoring it for years. Ever since old Regina Clover took over as Brentwell's councilor for open spaces.'

'Is that an actual job title?' Madeline asked.

Pete laughed. 'It is now.'

'Regina Clover. That's such a lovely name.'

'Suits her, don't it?' Dan said, cackling at Pete.

'Down to the ground,' Pete said.

Madeline was sure she was missing an in-joke, but she figured if she could just hang around long enough, she'd get up to speed. The dog, having lapped up all the water, picked up the bowl in her teeth and rested her head on Madeline's lap. Madeline, smiling, gave her a gentle stroke.

'She likes you,' Dan said.

'Isn't that Angela's favourite bowl?' Pete said.

'Oh god, is it?' Madeline said, grabbing the bowl and trying to pull it out of Milady's teeth, only for the dog to pull back, wagging her tail as though the bowl were a ball to be thrown.

'Come on, give it back!'

Milady wasn't having any of it. She shook her head, wrestling the bowl out of Madeline's grasp, then squatted down and crouched over it, holding it like a prized bone.

'Allow me,' Dan said, then gave a sharp click of his fingers. Milady let go of the bowl, tongue lolling as Dan picked it up and handed it back to Madeline, who stared at the teeth marks in the plastic with a look of horror.

'Angela's going to kill me....'

Pete grinned. 'Just playing with you, dear. It's IKEA.'

'You sod.'

Dan cackled, and patted Pete on the arm. Milady lifted her head and gave a genial bark.

'Sorry, couldn't resist. For what it's worth, though. Angela's favourite is the one with the ceramic sparrows on the side. She doesn't use that for anything.'

Madeline glared at him. 'Thanks, but I don't forgive you.'

'Free coffees whenever you come down south?'

'I'll think about it.'

Dan patted his knees. 'Right, better get these old bones home so I can rest up ready to scare Brentwell's delinquent youth again tonight. Thanks for the coffee, love. It was lovely to meet you, and I'm sure we'll bump into each other.' He winked his glass eye, making Madeline shiver. 'I look scariest in the fog just before dusk.'

'Thanks for the warning.'

As Dan took up Milady's lead and the pair headed off back the way they had come, Pete said, 'You know, the council didn't announce they'd hired a nightwatchman. They just put the rumour out that the park was haunted. Works a treat.'

'I still haven't forgiven you for the bowl thing.'

'I'll make your coffee extra sweet,' Pete said with a grin. 'Right, I'd better get back to it. Don't forget, any time you need something, just give me a bell.'

Madeline smiled. 'Thanks.'

Pete headed off back to his burger van. Madeline cleared up, then went into the café and started pottering around, trying to get her bearings. There were a few cakes left over from yesterday, but Angela had told her that the best time to bake was weekday mornings when the café was quietest, and the rest of the time she would have to learn how to do it around serving customers.

Through the window, Madeline could see that the park seemed empty. She wandered around the café, tidying things, adjusting placemats, straightening menus. On a shelf in a corner were a selection of paperback books and lifestyle magazines. Madeline pulled out a copy of an interior design magazine and began leafing through it.

The sun was beaming through the windows now, filling the café with beautiful autumn light.

I could get used to this.

A murmur of voices came from outside. Madeline looked up from her magazine as the doorbell tinkled. A middle-aged woman holding a flag that read Bolton Bus

Tours in red letters came bustling inside, standing back to hold the door as a line of elderly women began to file in.

'Okay everyone,' the tour leader said. 'We'll just stop here for brunch before we go over to the theatre.'

Madeline stared in horror as the café began to fill up. With shaking hands, she reached into her pocket and pulled out her phone and Pete's card, quickly stabbing his number into her keypad.

'Pete,' she said, as his cheerful voice answered. 'The bus tour lot just showed up. Help me….'

7

CRASHED TO EARTH

MADELINE STOOD OUTSIDE THE CAFÉ, the sun dipping towards the theatre behind her, and lifted a hand to wave as the coach from Bolton Bus Tours pulled away up the street. As soon as it turned out of sight, she staggered over to the nearest chair and slumped down. She gave her aching back a rub and sighed, then gave a defiant smile.

Baptism by fire and a half.

Pete had mercifully come to her aid during the first invasion, keeping the coffee machine ticking over as Madeline prepared twenty-five maple lattes and almost as many slices of cake with ice-cream. The old dears, filling the entire café with chatter, had seemed happy enough, so much so, that three hours later they had all showed up again after their theatre show had finished. By this time, Pete had already gone home, and Madeline, who had just begun to wonder about closing, had found herself back in action. Luckily, she had used the lull in custom over lunchtime to bake a couple of pies, both of which were now gone, into the diabetes-defying mouths of the hungry old dears. A few of them had patted her arm on the way out, one even donating a pot of hand cream, and another giving her a flimsy paperback book that 'my nephew wrote. We're all so proud.'

It was a quarter to six in the evening. Madeline had just turned around the CLOSED sign. Day one: survived. Who knew what day two might bring?

She went back into the café and tidied up. Angela didn't have a dishwasher, and as Madeline stared with dismay at the pile of dirty cups needing to be washed, she wondered whether she ought to hire someone to help. Angela had told her she was perfectly welcome to do as she wished, providing that she kept an eye on the bottom line.

After clearing up a little—deciding to leave the rest until the following morning—she went for a walk around Sycamore Park before going home. There was a scattering of people still around, several dog walkers, a handful of children in the playground, some old ladies throwing bread to the ducks in the pond. Old memories started to resurface, some good, some bad. Here, on this corner by the duckpond, she had been dumped by her first boyfriend. That she had been twelve at the time and he had broken up with her because her bike was more expensive than his made the memory more amusing than anything else. Madeline smiled at the way Martin Eggert had stamped his foot before climbing onto his bike and riding off, the chain rattling as it struggled to catch on the gears.

She passed the stump where she had shared her first kiss with Rory, refusing to dwell on it, but a little further on was the bench where they had held hands for the first time, looking out over the duck pond. An old couple sat on it now, their hands entwined, and for a moment Madeline felt such a sliding doors moment that she almost broke into tears.

It hadn't been all that bad, had it? After all, they had

been together for three years. They had both gone to the same school, but Rory, three years above her, had never so much as looked at her until she'd met him at Exeter University where he was a junior tutor. She had fallen for him over late-night coffee and long, often humourous discussions of cultural issues. He had still lived in Brentwell, commuting to Exeter by train, while Madeline had stayed in Exeter after graduation, living in an expensive flat with a couple of friends. She had worked a boring office job while she waited for some way to make use of her Modern Culture and Society degree, which had proved as worthless as the paper it was written on until she had started to look at work overseas.

Rory had been like one of those placid lakes filled with chemical runoff: beautiful and pristine to look at, but deadly if you got too close or dared get your feet wet. On the one hand he was a budding academic with one foot in the door at a prestigious university, but on the other he was a whiny, drunken mummy's boy who couldn't save time let alone money, wasting all his money in the pub or on unnecessarily expensive clothes and man toys. He had a Fender Stratocaster even though he only knew a handful of chords, one of those expensive radio-controlled cars that could go over thirty miles an hour, a small sailboat sat on a trailer next to his caravan, the awning that covered it caked with mud and dried leaves from years of disuse. He wore clothes that looked like regular clothes except that he'd bought them from expensive boutiques online, and handmade shoes that cost three hundred quid a pair which had never come within a mile of a brush and polish.

And after watching him fritter his money away, he had expected her to be happy about the chance to move into a caravan in his parents' garden.

No thanks, Rory. I'm good.

Yet there had been good times. Rory had been a listener, always ready to lend an ear to her problems. It had been Rory who suggested she look at working overseas, although she doubted he had actually thought she would go. Certainly, the tantrum he had thrown at her announcement suggested as much.

That had been eight long years ago. After going overseas, Madeline had cut off all social media contact with him, preferring to make a clean break. On the couple of times she had been home since, she had thought about dropping by his parents' old house, seeing if he was there. Jonas had suggested that he still lived in town, so what was stopping her? Maybe he had changed.

The old couple got up from the bench and wandered off, walking hand in hand. Madeline waited a few seconds, then claimed their old seat.

This was temporary. Angela would be back in the New Year, and Madeline would be off again on her next adventure. Part of the reason she had broken up with Rory had nothing to do with his juvenile behaviour. Once she had the travel bug, she hadn't wanted any ties. A clean break. And from the people she had met while travelling who were still in long-distance relationships with someone back home, her decision had been justified. Without exception they had been miserable; either pining to go back to their absent loved one, or wracked by guilt every time they did anything remotely exciting or interesting, while Bob or Michaella or Tristan or Olivia worked themselves into the ground back home.

Surely it wouldn't hurt just to see what he was like these days, would it? Just to say hello? They had both moved on. There probably wouldn't even be an attraction there. Perhaps the opposite: they would have grown so far apart that they were practically like strangers.

No, no, no. Don't do it.

She stood up, facing north, the direction she would need to go in order to get to Rory's parents' house.

Then, as though fighting against a magnetic force, she made herself step back and turn, heading south, away from the memories, away from the temptation, away from the chance to screw up her future—

'Watch out, you stupid hippy!'

She barely saw the bike as it came past her in a blur of colour, jerking to the side to avoid a collision. The rider let out a cry of horror as the bike pitched sideways, throwing him out of the saddle. He landed on a waist-high line of privet, bounced over the top and crashed down on the other side. The bike too struck the hedge, the front wheel sticking, the back wheel continuing to revolve, the spokes clicking gently as it slowed.

'Oh, so sorry!' Madeline cried. She hurried over to the hedge and leaned over. The rider was a man about her age, wearing an unfashionable tracksuit and sports shoes. She could only see his chin because the helmet had twisted in the fall to cover his face.

'Can you do something useful?' he snapped. 'Call an ambulance. I think I've broken my wrist.'

8

THE THERAPIST

'I THINK you'll be all right,' Jonas said. 'I mean, he can't sue you, can he? He wasn't supposed to be riding there.'

'It was after six p.m., so apparently it's allowed,' Madeline said, staring into space as her dinner went cold.

'He'd have to prove the exact time he fell off,' Jonas said. 'And it sounds like he was riding too fast.'

'The paramedic was scolding him about that,' Madeline said. 'His excuse was that he was late for work and decided to cut through the park instead of going around the outside. She said that hopefully he'd learn his lesson. I also heard her tell him it was only a sprain.'

'Well, that's good news, I suppose.'

'I still feel guilty,' Madeline said. 'I did kind of launch myself backwards into his way. I kind of deserved to be called a stupid hippy really. Do you think I ought to cut my hair?'

'Don't be silly. It's your hair, you have it how you want. The guy's an idiot. What on earth were you doing anyway?'

'I was … it doesn't matter now.'

'But otherwise it was a good first day?'

Madeline shrugged. 'Not quite what I was expecting.'

'It's a challenge, that's all. You'll do fine.'

'I hope so, but I'm not so sure.'

'My little girl can do anything.'

Madeline smiled. 'Thanks, Dad. I appreciate the support. I'm just not so sure, though.'

The next day it was pouring with rain, putting a literal dampener on things. She saw neither Pete nor Dan, nor had a single customer during the morning. On the plus side, it gave her a chance to clean up from yesterday as well as bake a couple of new pies. With the radio playing a little rainy day jazz, she slowly began to cheer up. She just hoped that today would be a little more normal.

She hadn't heard anything about the man who had fallen off his bike, but she hoped he was all right. She had given her details to the police, but she wondered if she should send him a card or maybe even visit him if he was still in hospital, perhaps to apologise. It still smarted that he had called her a stupid hippy, but it had been her fault really for not looking where she was going.

In the little kitchen behind the counter, Angela had a tall mirror hanging behind the door. Madeline stood in front of it, regarding herself. Her perma-plaits hung nearly to her waist, her hair parted in the middle. The round glasses she often forgot about made her eyes look bigger. Over a pair of dark blue jeans she had chosen a loose, floral apron with acorn and maple leaf designs, which probably looked a little cheesy. Still, it wouldn't be long before she was in sweaters all the time.s

Was she a hippy, though? She shrugged at herself in

the mirror. Overseas, she often got called "unique", whatever that meant. It definitely felt that she was judged more harshly back home in England, although one of the old dears yesterday had patted her arm and said, 'I wish I was young enough to pull off jeans that tight," with a tone of obvious envy.

The bell above the door tinkled. Madeline gave her shirt a tug, then headed back into the café.

A tall, elegant woman in a business suit stood by the counter. She was so made up that Madeline probably wouldn't have recognised her dressed down, her eyes and lips drawn in stern lines, her hair ruler straight, held to the sides by perfectly horizontal clips just above her ears.

'I'll take a honey-cashew nut latte,' the woman said.

'Honey, cashew nut, honey, cashew nut,' Madeline muttered to herself, wondering a) whether she had any of either, and b) if she did, where Angela kept it. To the woman, she gave a warm smile and said, 'Certainly. Why don't you take a seat?'

But the woman stood at the counter and continued to stare. One eyebrow lifted robotically, then her eyes suddenly widened.

'Oh, my heavenly wisdom,' she said. 'You're not Madeline Fellow, are you?'

'Ah, yes?'

'Wow, how remarkable. Of all the people to bump into. You don't recognise me, do you?'

As far as Madeline was concerned, she was talking to a complete stranger. She gave a shake of her head. 'Ah, I'm afraid my eyes aren't quite what they used to be.'

'I can see that. Really. Do you want to guess?'

'Ah, no?'

'It's *me.*'

'You?'

'Janine.'

'Ja—*nine*? Janine … Woodchuck?'

Janine's eyes narrowed. 'So, the taunting still runs deep. It's Woodfield. It's always been Woodfield. She gave a wide, sour grin, giving Madeline time to admire two perfect lines of bleached white teeth. 'I had them fixed,' Janine said.

'They look … nice.'

'No more, "Huh-huh, huh-huhs", behind my back,' Janine said, doing a pretty poor impression of a Disney character. 'No more taunting. No more having boys pretend to like me then run away screaming. No … more.'

'It sounds like you still have issues.'

Janine's eyes flared. 'I have no issues. No … more … Woodchuck.'

'Well, it's good to move on,' Madeline said, not sure what else to say.

'Yes,' Janine said. 'It is. And it's interesting that we've bumped into each other. It gives me a chance to tell you that I forgive you.'

Madeline started. 'Forgive me for what? I never bullied you. I don't remember really ever speaking to you.'

'No,' Janine said, narrowing her eyes, the forced beauty in her face sinister. 'You, like most of our class*mates*, didn't care to give the time of day to a bucktoothed girl sitting alone in the corner.'

'You didn't sit in the corner. You were on the third row back, by the wall, as I remember,' Madeline said.

'The metaphorical corner!' Janine suddenly roared, causing Madeline to make a step back. 'When you're bullied, you're in the corner every single step you take!'

'Well, like I say, I didn't bully you.'

'There are two types of bully,' Janine said. 'Active and

passive. There were those who did the taunting, and those who sat back and let it happen.'

'I'm sorry I never stopped anyone from bullying you,' Madeline said.

'Quite the apologist today, aren't you?' Janine said. 'It sounds to me like you have issues.'

'I—I—I don't have issues.'

Janine reached into her pocket and pulled out her purse. She withdrew a card and laid it down on the countertop.

'My card. If you need help—and I think you do —call me.'

'The coffee?'

Janine lifted a hand. 'I'll pass.'

Without another word she was gone, out through the door and away, her inappropriately tall heels clacking on the ground. Madeline just stared, wondering if the altercation had actually happened, or whether she was still dreaming from last night.

The card still lay on the countertop. Madeline picked it up and read it over.

Dr Janine Woodfield

Personal therapist

"Are you broken?"

Yes:: "But I can fix you"

Underneath was an address on Cloverdale Street, just a five-minute walk from Sycamore Park, along with a phone number.

It seemed that Janine had channelled her rough schooldays into a better life. Good for her. Had there been some truth in Janine's words, though? Did Madeline actually have issues that she hadn't really noticed before? Life on the road tended to be about living in the moment, and she had enjoyed the hell out of herself. But these long eight years of moving from place to place, was she actually running away from something, or even looking for something new?

An identity?

'You stupid woman,' she muttered, wondering whether she was talking to Janine or herself.

Outside, the rain had stopped. A couple of old people with a little Jack Russell on a lead were making a beeline for the café. Not wanting to dwell on her possible issues, nor the fact that the class weirdo was now an elegant—if stern—doctor of something or other, she began to root through cupboards, trying to figure out whether she had any honey or cashew nuts in stock, just in case.

9

THE PATIENT

BRENTWELL GENERAL HOSPITAL looked more like an office building than a place for sick people, a modern redbrick building with bright red doors, offering an ironic reminder of the colour of the substance many of those being rushed through the doors were likely to spill a little of, but it had some nice water features outside and a couple of pretty patios where family and well-wishers could drink coffee while waiting for their loved ones to either get better or die. As Madeline made her way up the steps to the main entrance, she caught sight of an elderly couple carrying a tray laden with large chunks of chocolate cake, and considered aborting her mission all together. As she stepped aside to let an ambulance crew with a stretcher push through the doors, the box she had brought nudged her in the ribs, reminding herself of why she had come.

Adam Wright. She had got the bike rider's name from the police, and the ward he was in from stalking him on social media. Apparently in addition to a sprained ankle, he had cracked a couple of ribs, meaning the hospital had kept him in for a while to keep him under observation.

Madeline, wondering if she was doing the right thing, asked at a reception desk, and followed the directions to Adam's ward.

He was lying in a bed near the window propped up on a pillow watching a wall-mounted TV, the only patient in the six-bed ward. She took a deep breath for her nerves and walked up to his bed.

'Um, hello.'

He looked up at her, frowning. Madeline hadn't got a good look at him before because he had been too animated with anger, but now that she did, she found he was easy on the eye, his body tight and strong. His eyes were a crystal lake blue, hair a wavy light brown. He looked at her, gave a slight shake of his head, and frowned.

'Hello? Do I know you?'

'Um, yes, I'm the hippy who knocked you off your bike.'

His eyes widened. 'Really? I didn't recognise you.'

Madeline lifted a hand. 'It must be the hat.'

His eyes narrowed. 'Yeah, maybe.'

Madeline offered a shy smile. He was still staring at her with a look somewhere between distrust and dislike.

'Ah, I brought you a get well soon present.'

She held out the box, but he made no move to take it nor even lean forward to get a better look.

'What is it? A replacement front wheel?'

Madeline winced. 'Um, no. It's a walnut and maple cake. I made it myself.'

His expression didn't change. 'That's nice. I have a nut allergy, but maybe you can give it to the nurses out there. The size of some of them, I doubt it would last long.'

She stared at him. He let out a huff and turned back to the TV, smiling thinly at a bland joke on the daytime quiz show he was watching. Madeline, stunned at how badly this had gone, was still standing there when he turned back again, lifting his hands.

'Four pounds fifty, please.'

'Excuse me?'

'Ticket price.'

Madeline frowned. 'What ticket?'

'For the freak show you seem so desperate to watch. Come on, four pounds fifty. Otherwise, get lost.'

Madeline had to force her feet to turn around, then her stiff legs to move, to propel her out of the room, away from Adam Wright's unpleasantness. By the time she had made it out into the corridor, she had tears in her eyes and her hands were shaking so much she could barely hold the cake. Like a zombie she staggered down the corridor, into a little waiting room at the confluence of four corridors, empty except for one young man leaning with his head back against the wall.

Tears dripped down on to the box as Madeline stood there, trying to remember which way she had to take to get back to the reception area. Neither her eyes nor her mind seemed to work; everything was a blur and she couldn't seem to get the words to equate into meaning.

'Are you alright?'

She looked around. The young man had stood up.

'What?'

'You're crying. Are you alright?'

She was crying too much to make out his face, and for a moment she thought it might be Adam, come to torment her.

'Leave me alone!' she shouted, flinging the cake at him, and fleeing into the nearest corridor. She ran and ran, past a handful of bewildered nurses and other hospital staff, not stopping until she had put several corridors and a couple of sets of stairs between them. Then, wiping her eyes and looking up, she realised she had by some miracle managed to find her way back to the entrance.

She must look terrible, but it was a hospital, not Harrods. She could be forgiven for having messy hair and bloodshot eyes. Nevertheless, wanting to throw off her humiliation, she straightened her back, lifted her head, and strode out through the doors, making it as far as the car park wall before she broke down again.

'It's all right, dear,' came a voice from nearby, and Madeline looked up to see a woman in a habit leaning over her. 'The Lord is indiscriminate in who he chooses, but rest assured, your loved one is now in a better place.'

'Huh?'

'Your loved one? The person you just went to see. He'll be living the better life in heaven already.'

Madeline scowled. 'He can go to hell for all I care. Him and his stupid bike.'

10

NEW BEST FRIEND

'IF I WERE YOU, I'd get on to old Regina Clover about getting some speed bumps put in,' Dan said, as Milady rested her head on Madeline's knees. 'That punk had no right riding his racer through here.' He sipped his coffee, wincing a little. 'You sure you put sugar in this?'

Madeline shrugged. 'Sugar, salt, sand, whatever.'

Dan winced again. 'Nah, I think it is sugar, but you probably want to double down a little.'

'I'm thinking of quitting,' Madeline said.

'Miss, don't you go worrying over one idiot,' Dan said. 'One snowball don't make a winter.'

'It might as well. I had two people complain that I was scaring their kids today. I tried to smile, but I just couldn't. He made me feel so worthless, and then I went and did exactly the same thing to someone else.'

'Well, why don't you go and say sorry to them?'

Madeline sighed. 'I have no idea who it was. I didn't even see them clearly.'

'Maybe that's for the best. Dan swallowed the last of

his coffee, then stood stiffly up. He patted his knee and Milady went skulking over.

'Right, thanks for the nightcap,' he said. 'I'd better be getting on with the guarding of this place. Don't you worry, if any more crazy bike riders come through, they'll get the eye.'

'Thanks, Dan.'

She watched the old man wander off across the park. It was nearly seven p.m. and she had stayed open an hour later in order to try to make up some of the business she had missed after lunch when she had closed for a couple of hours to visit the hospital.

Three days, and the honeymoon period was well and truly over. For most of the morning she'd been waiting for someone to show up, only to be inundated on her return from the hospital, as though they had all been waiting outside in the bushes, ready to jump out and scream 'coffee, coffee, coffee!' at the top of their voices. She had run out of walnuts, hazelnut topping, marshmallows, and whipped cream. She had got three orders wrong and overcharged one customer by mistake—only realising after they had gone, leaving her worried that they would return tomorrow to complain.

Angela had told Madeline that she could run the business in her absence how she wished, as long as she stuck to a few core principles and kept the regular customers happy. So far, apart from Dan and Pete, both of whom had stopped by regularly to see how she was getting on, she didn't seem to have anyone. Certainly, no one had come back twice that she could remember.

Around the back of the café, Angela had a little garden. Mostly flowers and herbs, it had been created on top of what had probably begun life as a gravel-covered nothing space a couple of metres wide between the café's rear wall and a tall iron fence that marked the outer edge of the grounds of the city library next door. Into that narrow corridor, Angela had inserted trellises and flowerbeds, a small rockery, stepped lines of pots filled with herbs, and even a couple of hedgehog boxes. A cast iron arch strung with pink, red, and yellow roses gave entrance to a den-like place, a little metal table and a couple of chairs on a circle of paving stones just wide enough to accommodate it, ringed on all sides by shrubs and flowers, few of which Madeline could name.

Angela hadn't specifically requested that Madeline maintain her garden, but Madeline found it comforting to pick the weeds out of the flowerbeds and trim back the excess growth on some of the shrubs with a pair of clippers she had found in a box inside the café's front door. It was easy to forget her troubles when she was hidden in this little space, so now, with the weight of the catering world, not to mention the wrath of all racing bikers everywhere, feeling firmly on her shoulders, she got down on to her knees and began to pick bits of grass out from between the paving stones, making a little pile on the path beside her.

She was just reaching under a hydrangea with huge, pink flowers to get at a stray piece of bramble, when she heard a little mew.

'Huh?'

She parted the clumped flowers, and there it sat, backed up against the central core of the bush, its claws dug into the earth, its ears flat against its head, shaking as though about to be snatched and eaten by some ghastly giant. It had a calico colour pattern, mottled with black, white, and ginger patches. The left side of its face was ginger, the right black, and the middle was a white triangle.

Beautiful green-blue eyes stared at her with a look of absolute terror.

I don't like cats. I really don't like cats. But … it's so cute.

'Hello,' Madeline whispered. 'Where's your family, then? They haven't left you behind, have they?'

The kitten gave a weak little mew, as though to say, 'Please don't eat me.'

Madeline leaned forwards, reaching out a hand, but the kitten just pushed its back up against the bundle of hydrangea stalks and for her trouble Madeline received a face full of flowers still wet from overnight rain.

'How are we going to get you out of there?'

The kitten gave another weak mew. It tried to back up further, but had nowhere to go. As it pushed against the hydrangea stalks, it had unwittingly enclosed itself at the same time.

It looked weak and helpless, but Madeline knew how fast the things could run if need be. She gently shifted, shouldering the branches with their cumbersome flowers aside, pulling her knees up in preparation to lunge forwards. When she was certain she was ready, she pushed with her feet, hoping to scoop the kitten up before it had a chance to get away. As she kicked out, however, one paving slab came loose under her feet and instead she scrambled sideways, completely missing the kitten and instead getting caught up in the hydrangea's branches. The kitten, seeing its chance to escape, scampered past her, actually climbing up over her back to get out from under the bush. By the time Madeline had twisted around, it was out by the patio, underneath one of the chairs.

It didn't move as she climbed out and brushed herself down, frowning at the muddy scuff marks on the knees of her jeans.

'Look, if you're going to make a fool out of me, I'm

not going to help you,' Madeline said, sitting up. The kitten crouched, ears flattening again as it hissed at her. 'And you can pack that in as well.'

She shuffled forwards. The kitten backed off, but as it did so, she noticed a slight limp on its front side.

'You can make this easy, or you can make this difficult,' Madeline said. 'But you're not in the best of shape and you're all alone. I think you need a little help, don't you?'

The kitten mewed at her again, calling for help yet afraid at the same time. Moving slowly, Madeline twisted around, preparing for another capture attempt. The kitten lowered its head in a gesture of submission.

'Just stay there,' Madeline whispered. 'Just stay—'

As she pounced, the kitten scarpered, racing in its limping way through Angela's little garden and around the side of the café. As Madeline reached the building's corner, she saw it, limping towards the park's northern gate. Beyond it, cars sped past, oblivious to the fragile little life about to come rushing into their midst.

It felt like a lifetime ago, but Madeline had once come third in the All-Devon Cross-Country Championship. She'd got lucky, the girl in front of her slipping up just short of the line to let Madeline squeeze into a medal position, but it was still one of her proudest achievements. It had been years since she'd even run for a bus, but now she channeled her old energy, set herself, and bolted after the kitten as it limped towards the street.

She had just reached the gates when it dropped down off the pavement. Madeline looked up at the groan of an engine, and saw a bus bearing down. She closed her eyes, summoned one last burst of speed, and dashed into the road, reached down and scooped up the kitten in one fluid motion. Then she looked up, waiting to die, only to see the bus lurch to a stop mere metres away. The horn blared, and the driver leaned out.

'Get out of the road, you crazy cat lady!' he shouted. 'Next time I'll flatten both of you!'

Clutching the struggling little kitten to her chest as she stepped back out of the road, Madeline resisted the urge to shout something abusive in return. At least his attitude was justified this time, she thought. Even if a little sympathy for a poor, helpless kitten wouldn't have gone amiss. The poor, helpless kitten that was currently trying to claw a hole in her stomach.

'I think it's time we had a look at you,' she said, pulling up the bottom of her sweater to wrap it around the kitten. 'And perhaps find you something to eat.'

Maybe it understood, or maybe it was the comforting warmth of her hands through the wrapping, keeping it safe, but the kitten stopped struggling. And a moment later, vibrating against her stomach like a miniature engine, the kitten began to purr.

RUBY

Jonas had a cat allergy, so Madeline couldn't take it home. Instead, she carried it back to the café, into the kitchen where Angela had an easy chair in the corner, then sat with the little thing nestled on her lap.

It's initial fear of her had quickly passed, and now it sat contentedly, purring under her hands as she smoothed its fur with gentle strokes. It was skin and bones, weighing barely more than a handful of rice. As she held it, it licked at her fingers, suggesting it either liked her or was developing a taste for human flesh, but aware it was probably hungry, Madeline carried it around the kitchen while she hunted for something suitable for it to eat.

She remembered reading somewhere that cow's milk probably wasn't suitable, but in any case, she had run out, and the variety of sugary goods and leftover pie didn't feel appropriate.

It was too late to take the kitten to the vet, but the Tesco Metro up on the High Street would be open, so she carried the little kitten over to Dan's portacabin at the south end of Sycamore Park, where the elderly nightwatchman was watching WWE on a small TV with Milady lying over his feet. As Madeline opened the door and leaned inside, he sat up, slamming one fist into the other palm and brayed, 'Oooh, tombstone!' at the TV. Milady lifted her head and let out a weak bark of support.

Dan was happy enough to look after the kitten for a while. Allaying Madeline's fears that Milady would either eat or terrify it, Dan held the little kitten out to the dog, which gave its head a sniff, then a lick, then a shove with her forehead. Nodding with satisfaction, Dan set the kitten down between Milady's front paws. Both the dog and kitten looked perfectly content.

'Nothing to worry about,' Dan said. 'Right. Cage match up next.'

An hour later, Madeline returned, laden with kitten milk formula, blankets, and a cardboard box. Dan had to go out on his rounds, so she wrapped the kitten up in a blanket and carried it back across the park to the café. Mixing a little formula with some warm water, she sat in Angela's easy chair and fed the kitten with a spoon. Then, after tuning the radio to a mellow jazz station, she settled down with the kitten nestled on her lap. She had planned to wrap it up in blankets and leave it in the box overnight, but after it had fallen asleep on her lap, she couldn't bring herself to move it. Glad she hadn't drunk too much coffee in the afternoon, she let the little fluffball's gentle purring soothe her, and before she knew it, her eyes were drooping, and then….

….she awoke with a desperate need to use the toilet. Through the café windows, a grey light was streaming in, marking it as sometime just before dawn. On a worktop beside her, her phone flickered with new messages. Even though she had texted her dad to say she might have to stay at the café "due to an emergency" it sounded like he was pretty worried. She called him, waking him up, muttered something about being sorry and that she'd be over for breakfast.

But where was the kitten? Suddenly panicking, she looked around, but saw no sign of it. Terrified she would never find it among the clutter of the shop, she got up, trying to ignore her aching bladder, and peered under counters and tables. Then, to her relief, she heard a weak mew coming from the door.

It seemed the kitten needed to use the toilet too.

She took it outside, let it relieve itself in a flowerbed, then took it back into the café and put it into the box while she sorted herself out. Feeling much better, she scooped it back out and sat down with it on her lap.

'We need to give you a name,' she said.

The kitten gave a little meow, as though to say it agreed.

'Hmmm, let's just check,' Madeline said, lifting up the kitten's tail. 'Okay, so it looks like you're a girl. What do you think would be appropriate? Fluffy? Tinkerbell?' The kitten seemed unimpressed by any of the options, continuing to purr in Madeline's lap. 'How about Butterscotch? Walnut? Or what about … huh.'

The kitten meowed.

'Sorry, that wasn't the option. It's autumn, isn't it? And I found you in autumn, so it seems appropriate to give you an autumn kind of name. How about Hazel? My grandmother's name was Hazel. And she was very nice, so I think that would fit. What do you think?'

The kitten pushed its head against the palm of Madeline's hand.

'Okay, Hazel it is, then.'

The kitten mewed.

'And it sounds like you're hungry again.'

Madeline mixed up a little of the kitten milk formula and set it down in a bowl for the kitten to drink. Even though it seemed a lot livelier than yesterday, however, it was still walking with a slight limp. Madeline frowned, shaking her head.

An hour later, she was sitting in the waiting room at Brentwell Animal Hospital, abbreviated over the door to B.A.H. At some point in the fairly recent past, some local illiterate had spray painted the word "hamburg" and an exclamation mark beside it, both of which had been partially washed off. As Madeline entered, a teenage receptionist with jet black hair, nose rings, and eye liner that made her eyes looked like black pits of hell raised her head and said, 'Welcome to Bah!' in an imposing voice which had two old ladies, one with a pug and the other with a chihuahua, rolling their eyes.

'Oh, Caroline, do stop it,' the one with the pug said.

'Uh, hello,' Madeline said. 'I found this kitten. Can I have her checked, please?'

'She's a stray?'

'I assume so.'

'No collar or microchip?'

'No, and I have no idea.'

'Okay, take a seat.'

Madeline sat down on a chair with Hazel nestled into her lap. Rather than sit still, though, Hazel seemed full of climbing spirit, attempting to scale the mountain top of her head while the two old ladies looked on with amusement.

'She's a lively little thing, isn't he?' the woman with the pug said.

'Yes, very much,' Madeline said. 'I just found her last night, round the back of my café.'

'Oh, you run a café?'

'Well, it's not technically mine. I'm the manager. Do you know the Oak Leaf Café by the northern gate of Sycamore Park?'

'Oh, Angela Dawson's place?' The woman leaned across and patted the other woman on the knee. 'Oh, Flora, we must stop in for a coffee once Brutus and Maximus have shaken off these worms.'

Madeline, who had been just about to pat the pug on the head, hastily withdrew her hand.

'Yes, what a lovely idea, Margaret. How are you enjoying it, dear?'

Madeline smiled. 'Oh, it's nice. A struggle at times, as it's just me in there on my own.'

'Why don't you hire someone to help out?'

'Ah, I don't know. I'm only the temporary manager while Angela's overseas.'

'I'm sure she wouldn't mind.'

Angela had actually told Madeline she could hire staff if she wanted, as long as she kept an eye on the bottom line. And having struggled with a couple of bus tours, not to mention constantly running out of things because she was too flat out to keep track of stock, she had to admit it would be a good idea.

'I'll think about it,' she said.

'Angela always used to hire students,' Flora said. 'Give them a bit of discipline, you know. Can't be all dancing and boys.'

Madeline cringed. 'No, I suppose not.'

'Caroline, dear,' Margaret called to the receptionist, who was staring at her iPhone. 'Don't you have any friends looking for a part time job? You know, in between all the drinking and bonking?'

Caroline didn't miss a beat. 'I'll ask around,' she said.

Hazel had got stuck in one of Madeline's plaits, and was swinging back and forth while trying to get her tiny claws into Madeline's left ear. As Madeline reached up her left hand to pluck Hazel free, she felt a wet sensation on her other hand, and looked down to see the pug licking her fingers.

A door opened beside the reception desk, and a man in a mask leaned out. 'Miss Fellow and Hazel, please.'

Madeline scooped Hazel into her hands and hurried into the consultation room, happy to leave the women and their dogs behind.

The vet, wearing a greenish-blue surgical gown and a face mask, frowned at Madeline as she put the kitten down, then tilted his head and let out a little chuckle. The strip of face she could see looked younger than she expected from a vet. He also looked vaguely familiar, but Madeline, wondering at what point she should mention the possibility of de-worming medicine for adults, couldn't quite place him.

'Who do we have here, then?'

'This is Hazel,' Madeline said. 'I found her last night, around the back of my café.'

She explained the circumstances of her discovery, leaving out the embarrassing chase and the near miss with the bus.

'Well, she looks pretty robust,' the vet said. 'You said she was running with a limp?'

'Yes. On her left front leg.'

The vet lifted Hazel, who mewed and batted his hand with one tiny paw. He turned her over and peered closer.

'She has a splinter,' he said. 'Don't worry, it's an easy fix.'

A few minutes later, Madeline emerged with Hazel in her arms. The vet had given her an injection, checked there was no microchip, removed the splinter, and armed Madeline with a bag of special formula for kittens, which he said would sort her out. She had to bring Hazel back for a checkup in a week's time.

She was feeling pretty buoyant when she got back to the café. The park seemed quiet, just a handful of dogwalkers and joggers, a few mothers with pre-school aged children. The sun was high above the trees, and the air had a light chill, a refreshing scent of recent rain.

As she went to open the front door, a girl she hadn't noticed before stood up from one of the picnic tables and slid a phone back into her pocket. She had hair dyed aquamarine blue tied back into a ponytail, with two orange strands hanging down either side of her face. She wore a black t-shirt with TURN OFF YOUR STUPID PHONE written in aggressive red lettering across the middle, black jeans, black shoes. A nose ring and too much makeup left Madeline unsure whether she was pretty or some sort of gothic art project.

'Hello,' the girl said. 'Are you Madeline Fellow?'

'Yes? Can I get you something? If you just hang on a minute, I'll open up—'

The girl beamed a wide smile and stuck out a hand littered with signet rings. 'I'm here for the job,' the girl said. 'My name's Ruby.'

'The job?'

Ruby grinned. 'Yes. My mate Caroline sent me a message to say you were hiring. Ignore the t-shirt. It was a gift.'

'I'm not—ah … hiring—' Madeline began, just as a tour bus pulled into the car park outside the theatre, dozens of old women peering expectantly out of the windows. '—but I might be right now … Can you make coffee?'

Ruby beamed again. 'Of course I can. I've been fired from every coffee shop in town.'

12

NEW FACES AND OLD

BY THE TIME the tour group had gone off to the theatre, leaving the café a sea of empty cups and plates, Madeline had promised herself never to judge a book by its cover again.

Not only was Ruby really good at making coffee, but she had a manner with the customers that defied all logic considering her somewhat odd appearance. Even those few customers who appeared a little unnerved by her cartoonish hair were converted by the time she had taken coffee over to their table, stopped for a chat about the weather, or complimented them on their hair or clothing. It made Madeline wonder quite why she had been supposedly fired by all of Brentwell's other coffee shops.

'Well,' Ruby said, holding up a hand as they sat together on two stools by the counter, the last customer of the morning rush having just gone out of the door. 'Number one … the manager asked for a date three times in the same day. He was proper old, at least thirty. The third time, I yelled "No means no!" into his face, and stamped on his foot.'

She had accompanied the explanation with an actual shout and a crack of her boot on the floor. Madeline flinched.

'That's understandable, I suppose.'

'So yeah, I got sacked. Second one, I sold these cakes off at half price to some homeless guy. The manager—who'd also asked me out on a date and I'd said no—got the hump, saying I shouldn't sell something with so much sugar to someone with so few teeth. I told him that if he looked closely, he'd see the man had dentures anyway, but that he never looked closely at anyone because he was a shallow turkey and an a—'

'Right,' Madeline said quickly. 'So you got fired?'

'Uh-huh.'

'The third one?'

'What third one?'

'You held up five fingers.'

Ruby smiled. 'Oh, those were just embellishments, to make the story more interesting. I did actually work at a third place, but I quit because the money wasn't so good.'

'So you've only been fired twice?'

'Yes.'

'Well, that's a relief. Consider yourself hired, if you want to be.'

Ruby beamed. 'Great. I'll start today.'

'You already did. Just let me know what hours you're available and we'll make you up a schedule.'

'Just one thing,' Ruby said. 'I mean, you might be a swinger, or whatever, but no asking me out on dates. You're way too old.'

'I'm not going to ask you out on any dates,' Madeline said with a smile. 'And I'm thirty-two. That's not old.'

'I'm nineteen. You could literally be my mum.'

'Only just. I could also be your older sister.'

'From a remarriage?'

Madeline just flapped a hand. 'I think it's okay if I just be your boss.'

'That's good. I have a couple of fisher toys anyway. I don't have time for anything more complicated.'   .

'A couple of what?'

'Fisher toys. Guys fishing for a date.' As thought to emphasise the point, Ruby's phone pinged. 'That'll be one of them right now.'

'And you date these guys?'

Ruby shook her head. 'Of course not. I just let them think I'm interested. I like to see how keen they are.' She grinned. 'Landing a fish is an art form. Check this out.' She opened her phone, displaying a message from someone called Mike (the guy at the O2).

Can you come up to London next weekend? I got VIP tickets for Foo Fighters.

Ruby opened the reply box and tapped a few random letters, then deleted them again and did the same.

'What are you doing?' Madeline said.

'I'm fishing,' Ruby said with a grin. 'He'll see this little box appear to say I'm replying. Then when I don't send, it'll drive him mad wondering what I'm going to say.'

Her phone pinged again. Ruby held it up and grinned. 'See?'

I'll pay your train fare.

'Wow, he's keen. Isn't that a bit … unfair?'

Ruby rolled her eyes. 'Off-peak return and he'll probably use his rail card. Unfair would be an Uber from Brentwell and an AirBnB in Camden. Don't worry, it's just a game. I don't even like Foo Fighters, plus I have a test on Monday. Do you have a boyfriend? I mean, a man-friend.'

Madeline chose to ignore the dig at her perceived age.

'A boyfriend, no. I've been travelling for a few years. Not long enough in any one place.'

'But if you're back for a while, you might want one?'

'If I do, I'll be sure to ask you for advice.'

Ruby beamed. 'Really? That would be awesome. I've never had a project before.'

With Ruby working three weekday afternoons as well as Saturdays, Madeline finally began to get a handle on things. Ruby, despite regular threats of hangovers, all night raves, and random road trips, showed up on time, made good coffee, and was great with the customers, allowing Madeline time to get the hang of the business side of things. Ruby's presence began to attract a younger clientele, with the café suddenly becoming popular as an afternoon haunt for student types who'd sit in the window seats drinking maple and walnut lattes while poring over thick textbooks of biology and geography. And even when they had a prolonged week of mid-September rain, the café stayed comfortably busy, enough that Madeline felt she was making a success of the place without being run off her feet.

By the end of September, nearly a month after Madeline had taken over from Angela, the café was running like a well-oiled machine. A newly regular crowd was slowly growing, and people greeted Madeline with an easy familiarity she had thought she would never achieve. Hazel, too, having doubled in size over the last three weeks, had become popular, and slotted neatly into being the café cat, greeting customers from a chair by the door, occasionally wandering among the tables to give legs a comforting rub, even climbing into a couple of laps, particularly those of people who came alone, and had a certain loneliness about them as they sat in the window, peering out at Sycamore Park as the leaves slowly began to change. Some, whose faces had harboured a longing, a sadness, started to leave with smiles, and Madeline, got the sense that what she was doing for them was far more than serving coffee.

On October the first, Ruby showed up with bright orange hair.

'It's seasonal,' she told Madeline, who looked up from the counter and raised an eyebrow as Ruby took off her jacket and hung it up behind the door. 'October Orange. Like, that's actually the name of the colour dye they use.'

'So what was the last one?'

'September Sky. Although I'd had it all summer.'

'And in winter, what do you usually use?'

'Winter White. Although it makes me look like I've got a snowball on my head so I usually add a few streaks.'

Madeline nodded. 'As you do.'

'Is it okay if I get off a little early this afternoon? I have to dump my boyfriend.'

'Really? That's too bad.'

'He's outstayed his welcome.' Ruby shrugged. 'It happens. For our second date gift he bought me a CD.' Ruby spread her hands. 'I mean, how old does he think I am? Forty?'

'What CD was it? Maybe you could donate it to the café?'

'*Boyband Number Ones of the 2000s.*'

'Wow, I bet that's a thrill a minute.'

'He's trying to tame me. Wants to set me adrift in a sea

of blandness. He might as well put a collar around my neck and throw me in a cage in Brentwell Zoo.'

'Brentwell doesn't have a zoo.'

'Exactly. My very existence will be compromised.'

'He's probably a nice boy, though. You know, safe. Can't you give him a second chance?'

Ruby stared at her. 'Say you're pushing forward to an inswinger, it pitches on middle, then cuts away and just kisses your off-bail, you're still out, aren't you? You didn't need to have your stumps shattered by an inswinging yorker, because out is out, isn't it? Even just a little bit out is still out.'

Madeline just stared at her. 'Were you just talking about a sport? Because all I heard was something-something-something-something.'

Ruby rolled her eyes. 'Cricket? You're not a fan? I play for Milton Road in the Brentwell Evening League,' she said.

'You … play … cricket?'

'Yes. I open the batting.'

'Milton Road … Ladies?'

Ruby narrowed her eyes again. 'Men's. Although technically these days, it's mixed.'

'I know literally nothing about cricket.'

'Actually, we have the Sunday Cup Semi-Final this weekend. Why don't you come? It'll be an education.'

'I can't, not with the café.'

'The ground is only a ten-minute walk and the game usually finishes by twelve, one o'clock at the latest. Go on, you know you want to. You never know, you might meet someone. Loads of old guys play cricket.'

'I'm not old!'

Ruby leaned forwards, lowering her voice. 'Loads of *rich* old guys.'

'I think you need to start making coffee. Looks like we've got a couple coming in.'

As she went back behind the counter and pulled an apron over her head, Ruby smirked. 'You're just avoiding the issue,' she said.

The morning had been nice but the afternoon a rainy, foggy affair, turning Sycamore Park into the setting for a Sherlock Holmes mystery. The steady stream of customers tailed off, and Madeline started to wonder whether closing early might not be a good idea. She needed to take Hazel to the vet for some vaccinations, and Ruby was always happy to go home early, because 'You know, studying.'

As she stood in the open doorway, however, at just a little after four o'clock, looking out at the sodden patio with brave circles of dry underneath the table umbrellas which were not quite wide enough to protect the seats, she put one hand on the door, ready to pull it closed. At that exact moment, however, a figure appeared out of the fog: a tall man in a business suit. He carried a black umbrella in one hand, a briefcase in the other, his dress shoes clacking on the paving stones.

For a moment she thought he meant to continue around the gentle arc of the path towards the library and the theatre, but then he suddenly veered off and made a beeline for the café.

As he walked out of the fog, his face revealed, Madeline felt a knot in her stomach. She stepped back inside, waving for Ruby.

'There's a customer coming,' she said. 'Can you serve him. I really need to … go to the toilet. I think that second piece of carrot and caramel cake was one too many.'

Ruby scowled. 'Ah, thanks for the info. No worries, I've got this.'

Madeline managed to get back behind the counter and into the little staff toilet cubicle before the man came inside. With her ear pressed to the door, she heard him order, heard him say he would sit in the corner. Madeline's heart sank. That meant she either had to stay in the toilet for the next half an hour, or toughen up and face him.

And she wasn't sure she could do that.

She hadn't seen Rory at all since her return, and she had gotten used to it. But seeing him come walking out of the fog, looking all mature and stylish, had turned something inside her, something she had thought she had long ago left behind.

A longing, a craving, a little slice of heartache pie.

And maybe, just maybe, despite his tantrums and his attitude, she was still just a little bit in love with him.

13

REKINDLED FIRE

A LITTLE TAP on the door.

'Do you want me to call an ambulance? Or did you just run out of toilet roll or something?'

'Just … a couple more minutes.'

'It's been forty-five. I'm officially doing overtime. You know, I'm pretty sure I remember you saying that was triple pay. Or was it quadruple?'

'All right, all right, I'm coming out.'

But she didn't. She cracked the door, then her hand froze, not allowing her to move it any further.

Ruby's orange-framed face appeared. She looked like a giant, real life corn doll.

'There's a guy out here who's absolutely bang on for you,' she hissed. 'Like, you'd need to smarten up a bit and drop the hippy skirts, maybe cut your hair about half, but he's totally your type, and he looks about your age.'

Madeline sighed. 'He's three years older than me. I know exactly how old he is because he used to be my boyfriend.'

Ruby stared. 'You gave up that suit? Seriously? I mean,

I expect he's totally boring, but he probably drives a Merc. I wouldn't be seen dead with someone like that, but I'm talking about for you. Easy middle-aged life on the cards. Yoga, painting classes, and sitting in cafés like this, rather than working in one.'

'Excuse me?' came a familiar voice. 'Can I order one more?'

'He's not going away,' Ruby said, trying to pull open the door. 'Just swallow a can of toughen-the-hell up and get out here.'

Madeline took a deep breath. 'All right, I'm coming.'

Ruby went off to serve Rory. Madeline closed her eyes for a moment, steeling herself, then stood up, opened the door, and stepped out. She took two steps forward, turned left past a protruding wall, and there he was, standing in front of her.

'Huh? Oh, wow. Madeline? Is that you?'

Madeline just spread her hands. 'Me? Ah, yes, I suppose it is.'

'You work here?'

'I'm the acting manager. I was just doing … stock check.'

Ruby turned back, catching Madeline's eyes and smiling. 'Did you flush the toilet?' she asked.

Under the promise of double-time, Ruby took Hazel off to the vet for her vaccinations, leaving Madeline and Rory to talk in private. Madeline flipped over the sign to CLOSED, got herself a coffee, and sat down across from him. Outside, the fog had closed in again, turning the Oak Leaf Café into the only café left in the world.

'Of all the places to bump into you,' Rory said, giving

her that easy smile that had defined him. 'I mean, I haven't been in here in years. I was just passing through, figured it might be a good time to stop by for a coffee, and well, here you are.' He chuckled. 'Well, after a stock check.'

Madeline grimaced. 'I think I'm eating too much sugar.'

She told him about taking over as temporary manager in Angela's absence. He listened with that attentive way that she had always loved about him, his eyes rarely leaving hers, pausing for a couple of seconds after she had finished before replying, proving he was absorbing what she said. If anything, he was a better listener now than he had been before. He looked better, too. His hair was neater, his body tight and toned, his skin clear. He had obviously aged, but aging seemed to suit him.

'I work in the private sector,' he told her, when she asked what he did now. 'I'm sorry to have turned all boring and corporate, but I needed to grow up, really. I needed to do something mature. It might not be saving the rainforests, but I'm doing my part.'

'That's nice,' Madeline said. 'What exactly do you do?'

'I work in recreation,' Rory said. 'More specifically, accessibility. I create ways for more people than ever before to enjoy their leisure time.'

'That's kind of you,' Madeline said, not really having a clue what he meant. The sincerity in his voice was enough, though. 'Not everyone can save the rainforests, can they? But it sounds like you're doing your part.'

'Oh, I am,' Rory said.

Madeline stared as he drank the last of his coffee, then looked at an expensive watch and sighed.

'No rest for the wicked,' he said. 'I'm afraid I've got yet other corporate type meeting. Let's see if I can make these people happy.' He turned to her. 'It was lovely to meet you again, Madeline. I enjoyed our talk. If you don't mind, I'd love to stop by again sometime.'

'Anytime,' Madeline said, a little too quickly. Before she could help herself, she reached out and patted Rory's hand. He didn't react, but he looked down and smiled.

'It really was good to see you again.'

'And you.'

He picked up his briefcase and umbrella, and went out. Madeline watched him go, walking around the gentle arc towards the mosaic plaza and the children's playground beyond, but he soon became little more than a silhouette in the fog. Just before he faded out of sight, however, Madeline was sure he paused and looked back.

She was sitting in the corner table, staring at the space Rory had recently vacated when the door opened and Ruby came in, Hazel's carry box under her arm.

'You owe me fifteen quid,' Ruby said, putting the box down on the ground and opening the door. Hazel, mewing, came scampering out. She ran to Madeline's leg, inserted her claws into Madeline's flesh, and began to climb. Madeline, grimacing, scooped the little cat up on to her lap before too much laceration could take place.

'So sorry about that,' Madeline said. 'I got a bit … flustered. Thanks for taking Hazel.'

'You're in demand,' Ruby said with a grin.

'What?'

'Firstly, I didn't realise that was where Darren worked.'

'Darren?'

'Darren Smith, the vet. I mean, I knew he was a vet, but I don't have any pets, so I've never seen him in battle, so to speak. Not that kind. He opens the batting with me for Milton Road.'

Madeline found herself shaking her head again, struggling to process the rolling waves of Ruby's information.

'The vet is called Darren, and he plays cricket. And I'm in demand?'

'He asked where you were. I know he was wearing a mask, but I've seen that look when I turn down a run from the non-striker's end. He was kind of gutted.'

'The vet....'

'Yeah. He's cool, is Darren. A bit old, but you know, in a Dad-like way. He's all right. I'll hook you up this Sunday if you like.'

Madeline put up a hand. 'I'm good.'

'You've fallen back into the whirlpool of your ex?'

'The ... no, I'm ... I'm fine.'

'You know, the reasons you dumped him in the first place will still be there,' Ruby said. 'He might have concreted over them, but weeds will grow and all that. Even if he did look knife-sharp in that posh suit. Can you really sell your soul for a Merc?'

'Can I ... weeds ... concrete....' Madeline shook her head and squeezed her eyes shut for a moment. 'Am I still paying you for this?'

'Uh-huh.'

'All right, well, thanks for everything. Get yourself home and I'll see you tomorrow. Take a couple of bits of pecan pie if you're hungry.'

Ruby grinned. 'Boss, you're the best.'

14

TREATMENT

'Do you think I'm drinking too much wine?'

Jonas laughed. 'If you top it up before you finish it, it only counts as one glass. I think one glass might be enough, though.'

'Yeah, me too.'

'Are you sure you don't want to tell me what's wrong, dear? Is it the café?'

Madeline sighed. 'No, the café's absolutely fine. I have a cat, and a good part-timer, and the takings are great. Yesterday I had three people tell me they thought my coffees were as good as Angela's. Not nearly as good, but as good.'

'But not better?'

'I think Angela took things to a celestial level.'

'So you're doing pretty good, then?'

'Yeah. It's just … I need more wine.'

'You need to go to bed.'

Madeline yawned. 'Yeah, you're right.'

She had taken to getting to the café early, around about seven o'clock, long before they usually opened. She would let Hazel outside for the toilet and a little play, then put the kitten back inside while she went for a stroll around the park.

It was a fine morning, the sun just above the horizon, a few wispy clouds in the sky. The air had that delicious, chilly crispiness to it, and a light breeze had begun to take browning leaves from the trees, scattering them across the grass.

Madeline said good morning to Dan and Milady, making their last circuit of the park before going home, then bought a coffee from Pete's burger van, pausing to chat for a while before leaving him to serve the first of the morning's commuters.

Everything felt wonderful … on the surface. But just beneath the pristine waters, Madeline was struggling. There was an aching feeling in her stomach that she just couldn't shake off.

It had been a couple of days since Rory's appearance at the café, and Madeline had struggled to concentrate since. During any lull in custom, she had found herself standing by the door, peering out at the park, wanting him to come strolling along the path. And when he hadn't, she had struggled to function. She had messed up a couple of orders, been sharper with customers than they deserved. She needed to sort herself out, and soon. Only she didn't know how.

Then, half an hour before the café opened, she had just put down some fresh formula for Hazel when she noticed a little business card tucked underneath a placemat behind the counter. She reached down and pulled it out.

Janine Woodfield.

Before she could chicken out, she picked up the phone,

dialed Janine's number, and booked herself an appointment.

~

She got Ruby to cover the café while she went over to Janine's office. It was not far from Sycamore Park, on the fifth floor of a modern office building. A pretty reception area complete with tall house plants and a fish tank had a view of the back of the theatre.

The door to Janine's office opened and Janine appeared, immaculately groomed and dressed. Madeline could almost hear the rustle of catalogue pages as Janine stepped out of the business section into the hall. 'Ah, Ms. Fellow,' she said, as though they had never met before. 'Please come this way.'

Janine's office was smaller than Madeline had expected, no bigger than the average living room, filled with a large desk in front of a window and ringed with tall shelves loaded with large hardcover books. Madeline scanned the shelves and caught such titles as *How to defeat YOU: Overcoming Insecurity*, and *Growing Pride from a Seed: Discovering the Mind Inside*. Already feeling a little overawed, she nodded dumbly as Janine waved her into an easy chair, then sat down opposite in a black leather swivel chair. She crossed one gym-honed leg over the other and drummed her fingers against the armrest.

'You've made the first vital step today,' she said, before Madeline could speak. 'You've put your hand up, and admitted you need help. Tell me, how are you feeling?'

'A little hungry,' Madeline said.

'That's good,' Janine said. 'Hungry for more. Hungry for success. Hungry to overcome the hurdles in your life.'

'I could do with a sandwich,' Madeline said.

Janine leaned forwards. 'And therein lies the crux. A mystery package, a surprise, a step into the unknown. Your life has become bland, unfocused, and today you have come to me for a reset. Tell me, Ms. Fellow, if you could choose any sandwich right now, what would you choose?'

Madeline frowned. She'd been expecting deeper questions. 'I'd probably be good with cheese and pickle,' she said.

'Blandness and spice,' Janine said. 'My god, reading you is like reading a comic book. You're as shallow as a puddle, Ms. Fellow.' She leaned forwards a little more, until it looked like she might fall right off her chair. 'How about we go about establishing some depth?'

'Ah … depth?'

'Let me see if I can read you, fortuneteller like.' Janine narrowed her eyes. 'You were a middling student. You got average grades. You did a little bullying, but not enough to get truly accepted into the bullying crowd, while not being bullied enough to be part of the good old losers' club. You were so middle of the road that you'd walk down the central line on the way home. My god, people like you disgust me.'

'Really?'

'You've done nothing, have you? Nothing at all in your life.'

Janine seemed to be getting a little hot under the collar. Madeline tried to shrink back a little, wishing the cushions might fold around to protect her.

'Ah, I've been overseas—'

'But you were never really there, were you? Your mind was always right here, in Brentwell, craving for the resolutions you could only find in this very room—'

Janine slid off the seat, caught herself, and got back on. Her cheeks were flushed, a line of sweat under her brow.

'I'm not sure—'

'Exactly!' Janine thumped the armrest hard enough to make the chair shake. 'And that, Ms. Fellow, is the root cause of everything. Let me tell you a story. I used to be just like you: weak, unfocused, treading water, drifting through life.'

'I think I'm in love with my ex-boyfriend—'

'Don't interrupt. But then one day, after a particularly savage day of being bullied, I lifted my head, looked in the mirror, and told myself, "No more." I began that path of growth that led me to where I am today, standing before you, standing *over* you, Dr. Janine Woodfield, high earning, highly successful, career orientated, engaged to a wonderful, handsome man, owner of my own home, master of my own destiny—' Janine leaned forward. 'Tell me, Ms. Fellow, do you want to become just like me?'

There were two possible answers. Madeline went with the one she suspected Janine wanted to hear.

'Ah, yes?'

Janine nodded. 'Good. I thought so. I'll see you next week at the same time.' She stood up, wheeled her chair back behind her desk, picked up a little lime-green watering can and began feeding a line of pot plants. 'Be sure to tell Edith on reception whether you'd like to pay weekly or sign up for a package deal,' she added, not looking back. 'Ten percent discount on bookings of ten sessions of more.'

With a shrug, Madeline stood up and went out. In reception, a smiling girl in her early twenties asked her for seventy-five pounds.

'But the website said twenty-five,' Madeline protested.

The girl gave her a sympathetic smile. 'But this was an initial consultation,' she said. 'Wherein Dr. Woodfield established your needs. Is the same time next Tuesday all right?'

'I don't think I need any more sessions,' Madeline said.

'In that case, it's one hundred and fifty,' Edith said.

'What?'

'Initial consultations with the doctor are billed at half price when a full treatment course is ordered,' Edith told her.

Madeline sighed. 'I guess I'll see you at the same time next week, then.'

She was still feeling a little flat when she got back to the café, but quickly galvanised herself into work mode when she saw that all the outdoor tables were full, and a gaggle of conversation was coming through the open café windows. She hurried inside, waving at a smiling Ruby, who wiped a theatrical hand across her brow.

'Bus tour came in,' she said, then nodded at a girl carrying a tray of coffees over to a table of old ladies. She was pretty, a few years younger than Madeline, in her mid-twenties, perhaps. She talked to the customers with a casual ease, and when Madeline noticed one of them patting the engagement ring on her finger, she couldn't help but feel a little pang of envy.

'That's Lily, Pete's daughter,' Ruby said. 'I hope you don't mind. I recruited her for the afternoon. I offered her free lattes for the next month.'

'Hi,' Lily said, returning to the counter. 'You must be Madeline. Ruby said you were desperate. I was over at thRory, covering for Dad, as he has a bit of a cold.'

'Thanks so much.'

Lily smiled. 'Anytime. I'd better get back to thRory if

that's okay. Not much going on at this time of day, but usually around three we get a few early commuters.'

'No problem.'

'Good luck.' Lily glanced over her shoulder at a group of old men in the middle of a heated conversation. One was on his feet, jabbing a finger at the others. 'A bit of a storm going down at the moment. I'd let them argue it out.'

'What happened?'

Lily's smile dropped. 'The theatre's selling off its free car park to a private company.'

15

RECONNECTING

'THOSE COMPANIES ARE the scum of the earth,' Ruby said, sipping a coffee as she sat with Madeline at one of the outside tables, after the tour group had departed. 'It's like a tax inspector and a traffic warden got together and spawned.'

'Spawned?'

'Like, had a whole load of eggs. Honestly, my dad says they're right up there on the league table of scumbags with debt collection agencies, temp companies, and zero-hours contractors.'

'You seem to know all about it.'

'My uncle is a delivery driver for one of those big companies. If he's thirty seconds late, he gets fined double the delivery fee. Honestly, someone needs to dig a massive pit and throw all these companies inside. It's like, how can you live with yourself?'

'You should run for council.'

Ruby tugged a strand of brightly coloured hair. 'I just might.'

'So a notice went up?'

'Yeah. The theatre is in contract negotiations right now. The company have posted a proposal up by the entrance gates.'

'I think I'll go and have a look. Will you be alright for few minutes?'

'If you hear me screaming, that means another bus tour has come in.'

∾

The notice was posted to the gate by the car park's entrance.

Snide and Company Parking Contractors: Proposal: a redevelopment of the current Brentwell Theatre car park

How this benefits you
Approximately 20% more spaces
Better security
Capital raised to aid local businesses
Investment back into the surrounding area

It didn't sound too bad to Madeline. When she returned to the café, however, Ruby was quick to point out the true meanings behind each bullet point.

'Wow, you've been overseas too long,' Ruby said. 'I suppose they don't have these scumbag contractors where you were living?'

Madeline shrugged. 'I never had a car,' she said.

'More spaces means they'll make the current ones smaller. And you know, if you go even an inch over the line, you get fined. My dad got one from outside Brentwell Station. And you can't dispute it because their customer service is a machine. Better security means they'll put up a gate so you can only park there when they choose, and guess what? If you're caught inside after that gate closes, you'll get fined.'

'Okay….'

'Capital for local businesses … well, guess what the new local business is? Themselves. Scumbags. And investment back into the surrounding area probably means their filthy inspectors will buy the odd coffee while laughing gleefully at all the pensioners they've managed to fine that day.'

Ruby was seething, practically bouncing up and down with rage. Madeline patted her on the shoulder. 'You really should run for council,' she said. 'But while you're considering it, perhaps you should go home early.'

Ruby nodded. 'Thanks, Boss. Are you still up for cricket on Sunday? Don't forget, I'm going to introduce you to Darren.'

Madeline smiled. 'Sure, why not?'

It was a lovely evening, the sun dipping into the trees on the west side of the park, no wind, and the air unseasonably warm, so Madeline kept the café open a couple of hours longer than usual. Dan, arriving for work, stopped by for a slice of cake and a coffee, Milady looking on with bemusement as Hazel used the dog as a climbing frame. On the subject of the car park, Dan was reticent. Not being a car owner himself, he didn't really have a finger in that argument, he told her, but he'd overheard a couple of bus drivers loitering around while their groups were in the theatre talking about how their companies would likely refuse the parking fees.

'And you know what that means, don't you?' he said. 'No customers, no theatre.'

The light was starting to fade, and Madeline was just packing up to go home, when a familiar voice said, 'Hey.'

Her heart skipped a beat. She swallowed before she looked up, then turned to see Rory standing nearby in a snappy business suit, an umbrella hooked over his arm despite the cloudless sky.

'Hey, Madeline. I didn't expect to find the café still open. It's pretty lucky. I'd love a quick cappuccino or something.'

Her heart plumed with warmth. 'Sure.'

The day's heat was finally starting to give way to the evening's cold, so they went inside. Rory took a seat at the counter, watching her as she made a coffee for him, and one for herself, because … just because.

'You know, it looks like you've made a real success of this place,' he said. 'I'm happy for you, I really am.'

Madeline's cheeks flushed. *What's wrong with me? It's like I'm fifteen again.* 'It's only temporary,' she said.

'That's a real shame,' he said. 'I'd love it if you stayed around. It would be great for us to reconnect, wouldn't it? I … missed you.'

Reconnect. Was that a modern way of saying get back together?

A month ago, she wouldn't have heard of it. Rory was metaphorically dead and buried, Rory was the past. But that had been the old Rory. This new, mature Rory was a different matter, almost like an improved, updated model of a classic car. All the good parts remained, but all the parts that had frustrated, worried, and even angered her … were gone.

She made the coffees and brought them over to the counter, adding a couple of slices of chocolate cake. Looking at the set up, it could almost be a first date.

'You know,' Rory said as she sat down beside him, 'It's weird being in here, isn't it? I mean, when we were a couple, we could barely afford it, could we? Do you remember that time we shared a hazelnut mocha over by the duck pond, taking it in turns to take a sip, and then I got that last bit of cream on my lip, and you….' He chuckled. 'Remember that?'

Madeline's cheeks burned, and it was as though the last eight years had never happened. 'I kissed you to steal it back,' she said.

Rory smiled. 'Good days.'

'Yes.'

Madeline looked down at her coffee. Part of her wished she'd never left, that she had forfeited the last eight years of adventures to stay here in Brentwell and observe the evolution of this man firsthand.

'Then there was that time we went halves on a piece of almond fudge cake. I let you have the top with all the icing, which I had the dry bit at the bottom.'

'And you made me feel so guilty.'

'I had to dip it in the coffee.'

'Yes, that's right.'

The air blowing through the café, so warm and nostalgic, briefly paused as a slightly different version of the memory raised its head, of Rory moaning about how she hadn't saved him any of the icing, but Madeline shrugged it off. The rest was great. The rest of that day had warmed her heart.

'That was when we sat under the theatre's eaves and told each other our dreams, wasn't it?' Rory said. 'You told me you wanted to travel the world, and I said I wanted to be a scientist.'

Madeline looked down again. She had done what she had promised that night. But what about him?

'And here we both are, right back at the start,' she said.

Rory nodded. 'That's true. Isn't it amazing how things like that can happen? We were a million miles apart, and now we're sitting beside each other again.'

He was close enough that he could have leaned in and kissed her. Madeline waited, but the moment passed as Rory looked away.

'Has the café changed since we were teenagers?' he asked.

'Ah, I think so. It looks like they expanded the seating area a little.'

'How many can you get in here now?'

'We get bus tours of up to fifty. It's a real squeeze, but we just about manage. There's a stack of spare chairs out in the kitchen. I think thirty is about our safe maximum, although ten to twenty is plenty.'

'And you just serve drinks, or do you do food?'

'It's mostly drinks and cakes, but we do a few meal options. There are Ploughmans, and seasonal salads, pies with garnish. The café is technically vegetarian, so we don't do any meat dishes. Lots of quiches, things like that.'

'And do you do bookings?'

'Yes, of course. We don't get many, though.'

'Right.'

Rory was nodding thoughtfully, as though sizing something up. Madeline leaned forward, catching his eyes.

'Were you thinking of booking something? A work party, perhaps?'

Rory just shrugged. 'Maybe. I'll be in touch if so.' He

picked up his drink and finished it in one swallow, then stood up. 'Thanks so much, Madeline. I'd better go, though. Things to do and all that. I hope we can reconnect some more.'

That word again. This time, however, it felt empty.

'Do you want me to wrap up the cake?'

'Ah, sure.'

She went back behind the counter, fetching a piece of waxed paper and a paper bag. She gently wrapped the piece of chocolate cake and handed it to him as he stood up, adjusting his business suit.

'I'll stop by again soon,' he said, as he headed for the door. 'It's so nice to see you again, Madeline. I'm looking forward to the next time.'

'Me too,' she said, a little too quickly, perhaps.

He opened the door, and she took it to allow him to leave. There was another brief moment where they were close enough that he could have kissed her, but after a pause that felt hours long, he nodded and muttered goodbye. Madeline stood by the door, watching him go. Just before he went out of sight around the corner towards the duck pond, he glanced back, saw her still watching, and lifted a hand to wave. Madeline's heart felt as soft as the fudge inside one of the cakes. She waved back, then closed the door, swooning back inside.

She felt almost drunk as she cleared the used cups and plates, then went through her usual closing routine. She was nearly done when a little meow came from the door. Hazel, fast asleep in a basket by the window for the last couple of hours, had finally woken up and decided she wanted to play.

'Come on, then,' Madeline said, twisting the sign to CLOSED just in case, then opening the door for the little kitten to get out. She followed Hazel outside, then closed the door behind her.

Hazel was getting big. Madeline had promised Tom, the park's caretaker, that she would keep a close eye on the little cat, in case Hazel got a little excited by the ducks around the pond, but Hazel seemed happy enough chasing the dancing leaves as the wind picked up in the dusk.

'Don't go so far,' Madeline called, as Hazel raced among the trees, twisting and rolling playfully, leaping to catch leaves drifting down through the air with an agility Madeline could only imagine.

The cat, excited by a moth fluttering among the trees, raced off in the direction of the duck pond. Madeline jogged along the path in pursuit, then reached down and scooped up the little kitten just before she could make a fateful dive into the reeds around the water's edge.

'I think you need to calm down a little,' she whispered, stroking the struggling, mewing thing as it wriggled out of her gasp and climbed up onto her shoulder. With Hazel seemingly happy to sit at the top of her human observation tower, Madeline took a few more steps towards the pond, noticing a group of ducks fussing about something on the riverbank. As she got closer, one of them claimed the hidden prize, lifting its beak to swallow down what it had found, only for it to break apart, showering the others with crumbs. A loud argument ensued, but Madeline had got a glimpse of what the ducks found so important.

A large slice of chocolate cake, discarded on the riverbank, still wrapped in a piece of waxed paper.

16

HEROISM

SHE DWELLED on it all evening, and all the next day, which was Saturday. The weather was warm and dry so they did a lot of takeaways, but around serving the customers, Ruby asked Madeline several times what was bothering her. Madeline just shrugged her questions off, however, unable to put her feelings into words.

Perhaps he had dropped it, or perhaps he really liked ducks. But with the wrapping as well? That was littering, wasn't it? Maybe he just didn't like chocolate cake, and Madeline had forced it on him. Perhaps it was her fault that it had ended up becoming a battleground for hungry ducks.

At the end of Saturday, Ruby asked her again if she was up for the cricket on Sunday. The café had a couple of lunchtime bookings, but Ruby promised the game would be over around twelve, and they could come to work together. Even so, Madeline was reluctant, preferring to wallow in her insecurities. As she turned the CLOSED sign on Saturday evening, having stayed open a couple of hours later than usual, long after Ruby had gone home, she stared out at the park, now gloomy with the sun long gone, and wished Rory would appear. If for no other reason than she could ask him why he had thrown the piece of chocolate cake away.

~

She drank too much wine over dinner that night, but she had to have mentioned the cricket match, because at seven on Sunday morning, Jonas shook her awake as he had so many times during her teenage years and told her to get herself out of bed.

Brentwell Cricket Ground was a ten-minute walk northwest of Sycamore Park. Madeline stopped in at the café to feed Hazel and clear out the cat's litter tray, then give her a quick run outside. With the kitten settled again, she headed up to the ground, just as the players and a handful of spectators were starting to arrive.

'Hey!' came a familiar voice as Madeline loitered awkwardly near the entrance. She spun around, and couldn't help but let out a surprised gasp. Ruby, Halloween-orange hair framed with purple lines, was standing behind her, dressed in cricket whites, a bat over her shoulder.

'There's fashion and then there's fashion,' Madeline said, shaking her head.

'We won the toss and chose to bat,' Ruby said.

'Which means…?'

Ruby swung her bat through the air in a dramatic swish. 'I'm gonna go open up a large pot of glue and hand out a pasting.'

'I can't wait.'

'Come on, let's go meet some of the guys.'

To Madeline's surprise, there were actually two other

girls on the team, one massive ginger-haired girl Ruby introduced as Ivy, "the best spin bowler in Brentwell", and a far lither woman called Margaret, who kept wicket. As Madeline tried to pause for conversation, Ruby, however, was keen to move on.

'Wait here,' she said, as they came to a white-walled clubhouse with a large scoreboard outside. Ruby disappeared into a changing room, leaving Madeline standing outside, feeling a little out of place among all the white-clad people. In her haste to be on time, she had thrown on a floral patterned blouse with a pair of jeans, and looked a little like a flower seller at a nunnery.

'Madeline, this is Darren, my opening partner.'

Madeline almost missed "opening", remembering it was a cricket term. The white-clad man standing in front of her smiled. He was in his mid-thirties, tall, fair-haired, with bright blue eyes. His smile was easy and kind.

'Hi,' he said. 'You're Hazel's cat-mother.'

'Huh?' *Oh.* 'Yes. That's right.' *Stop being so weird.* 'You're the vet, aren't you? Doctor Smith? Thank you for saving my kitten.' *Please, stop being so weird.* 'I'm afraid I didn't recognise you. I've only ever seen your eyes.'

Darren's smile dropped. 'You don't remember me, then?'

'Remember you? Of course—'

'From the hospital waiting room. You threw a cake at me.'

Madeline stared, openmouthed. As the wind gusted, she snapped her mouth shut, worried the wind might change and leave her stuck looking like a gormless idiot until the end of time. 'I … oh my god. That was *you*?'

Darren smiled. 'I managed to salvage some of it. Honestly, it was one of the best cakes I've ever tasted. I really wanted to say something when you came in to the vets, but the timing wasn't great. If it's okay by you, I'd love to come by for another slice sometime.'

'Ah, sure, that would be—'

'All right, everyone, listen up!' came a man's voice. 'We have a game to win. Darren, Rubik, get out there and get us a good start.'

'Got to go,' Darren said. 'Wish me luck!'

'Good luck!'

The opposition were already out on the field. Darren grabbed his bat and hurried out on to the field. As Ruby passed her, Madeline mouthed, '*Rubik?*'

'It's a long story,' Ruby mouthed back.

Madeline didn't know the first thing about cricket other than that you had to hit the ball as far as possible without getting caught, something like that. Ruby, despite her diminutive size, batted like a banshee, particularly after one man fielding close called her Pumpkinhead. After that, she smashed everything coming her way, and was out, caught on the boundary, for thirty-five, after facing only fifteen balls. She walked off with a scowl as the fielders clapped.

'Well batted, Rubik,' said the captain, patting her on the shoulder as she crossed the boundary edge. 'Five degrees to the left and that was six.'

'Got it, Dad,' Ruby said, scowling at Madeline, who gave her a polite clap. She disappeared into the changing room, reemerging a few minutes later having taken off her pads, and came to stand next to Madeline, who was clapping politely as Darren and the new batsman ran up and down.

'You did great,' Madeline said. 'That one you hit that bounced off the clubhouse roof … wow.'

'Yeah, nailed that one,' Ruby said. 'Guy standing in close there was doing my head in. I tried to take his off. Unfortunately he ducked.'

The man Madeline had established as both the team captain and Ruby's dad, turned towards them. 'Rubik, can you take over from Josh in the scorebox? He needs to pad up.'

'Sure, Dad.'

'So … Rubik?'

Ruby sighed. 'Tell no one.'

'Don't worry, your secret is safe with me … and both teams, by the look of things.'

'Dad's a math teacher,' Ruby said with a grim smile. 'When he was a teenager, he came third in an Olympiad. Solved that accursed cube in sixteen seconds. It was a regional record for twenty years.'

'That's pretty impressive.'

'Yeah, for him, maybe. School was a minefield. The only way I could survive it was by being so clever I created a circle of nerds around me like a wall to keep the rest of the kids out. She flicked a strand of purple hair. 'The rebellion came late, but when it came, it was mighty and fierce.'

'Good for you.'

'You want to come and help in the scorebox? I'll do the actual scoring. You can just flip the numbers over.'

'Sure, why not?'

In behind the tall plywood scoreboard was a cramped little room with a window underneath the numbers through which they could observe the game. Ruby marked down every ball in a complicated book, then instructed Madeline which of the levers above their head to pull in order to change the numbers on the outside.

'So,' Ruby said, once they were settled on a bench,

peering out at the game. 'What do you think about Darren?'

'Ah … he seems nice.'

'Nice? Is that it?'

'I didn't really speak to him.'

'He's totally smitten with you. At practice the other night, after he'd found out that I worked with you—sorry, *for* you, lol—he just kept banging on about it. Honestly, it was getting on my nerves.'

'Is he a bit weird?'

'He's a vet, of course he is. What kind of clown spends five years at university learning how to be hated by animals?'

'Well, I—'

'Only joking. Wow, look at that, he just hit a six!'

Ruby began cheering and banging the inside of the scoreboard. Madeline looked for the ball, but could only see a man climbing up into a hedge on the far side of the ground. After a couple of minutes of poking among hawthorn bushes and weeds, he held up the ball to a triumphant cheer from the other fielders.

'Darren's on forty-nine,' Ruby said. 'If he gets one more, he has to buy a jug.'

'A what?'

'A jug. A pitcher of beer. You get a fifty or a hundred, take five wickets, or five catches, you have to buy a jug in the pub after the game for the rest of us to share. Come on, Darren, just one more run….'

The bowler ran in. Darren took a horrid swipe, and his stumps exploded. There were cheers from the opposition, boos from the Milton Road players as Darren tucked his bat under his arm and started walking off. As Darren reached the boundary rope, theatrically shaking his head, there were a few ironic claps from the home team.

'Well batted, lad,' Ruby's father said, patting Darren on the shoulder as he passed him on his way out to bat.

'Jug avoidance!' Ruby shouted out of the scorebox window.

Darren gave her a shrug. 'It hit a divot,' he said with a smile.

Milton Road ended up with what Ruby considered a decent score of 175. Madeline poached a deckchair as Milton Road went out to field. She was just settling in for an hour of watching the opposition bat, when she noticed Ruby and her father in discussion by the boundary edge. Ruby was shaking her head, but her father kept glancing in Madeline's direction. In the end, Ruby came jogging over.

'Ah, you might have noticed we only have nine players,' she said.

'Isn't that how many you're supposed to have?'

'No, we're two short. Dad wants to know if you can field.'

'Field? Me?'

'Yeah. I've got a white t-shirt you can wear. Don't worry, we'll put you at fine leg, down behind the 'keeper. You probably won't have much to do. If the ball comes to you, throw it back to the 'keeper. And if it's in the air, catch it.'

'I've never played before.'

'I'll buy you a coffee.'

'From my own shop?'

Ruby grinned. 'Staff discount.'

Madeline stood up. Her heart was racing with nerves. She patted her thighs and grinned. 'All right. Why not?'

Five minutes later, she was standing behind the wicketkeeper on the boundary edge as the bowler came running in from the other end. She waited, expecting the batsman to either hit the ball or the 'keeper to catch the ball, but instead neither happened. The ball missed both, and came bouncing down towards her. Completely unprepared for the speed at which the ball was travelling, by the time she'd got a hand down, the ball was past her and bouncing over the boundary.

'Four wides,' the umpire shouted, holding his arms out to the sides as the batting team cheered.

'Get behind the ball!' Ruby's father shouted. 'We're three percent statistically more likely to lose now!'

Darren came running over from a nearby fielding position. 'Don't worry,' he said, patting her on the shoulder. 'When the ball comes, drop your calf along the ground, like this. It creates a barrier in case your hands miss the ball. Good luck.'

His eyes lingered on hers a little longer than was necessary, but Madeline found herself staring back. They were nice eyes. Kind. She was almost disappointed when he turned away.

Ruby had told her that fielding at fine leg was boring and that she would rarely touch the ball. In reality, the bowlers were erratic, Margaret, the wicketkeeper, could barely stop the ball, and a couple of decent batsmen insisted on hitting everything over the 'keeper's head in her general direction. And on top of everything else, every six balls the bowlers changed ends, meaning that Madeline had to run all the way to the far end of the field, while the rest of the fielders just shifted back and forth. By the time the game came down to the last six balls, with the opposition nine wickets down and needing just four to win, she was puffing, her palms aching from stopping the ball, her arms aching from throwing it back, and the sides of her calves smarting from every time the ball had slipped through her hands.

Despite everything, though, she'd enjoyed it, and now, with the game down to the wire, she felt as excitedly nervous as the rest of the Milton Road team.

'Keep it tight, keep it tight!' Ruby's dad shouted over and over again, clapping his hands together as the bowler ran in. 'Just keep it tight and we're in the final!'

The opposition's last two batsmen were both beginners, barely able to get bat on ball, and by time the last ball came around, they still needed three to win. The game was practically in the bag for Milton Road, barring some last ball miracle hit. As the bowler came running in, Madeline found her mind drifting to the café, wondering how many coffees her sore hands were likely to have to make over the afternoon. The sun had come out, the air was clear … it was perfect park and coffee weather.

'Catch it! Catch it!'

Madeline jerked back to reality in time to see the ball come sailing through the air in her direction. She barely had time to get her hands up before the ball was bouncing out of them, spinning away into the grass.

A groan came from the Milton Road players, a cheer from the opposition. Madeline felt her face prickling with shame. She had given the game away, lost the match at the last moment with a lack of concentration—

'They're running three! Get the ball back in!'

Madeline spun around, looking for the ball. It was a few yards away, lying in the grass. She dived for it, coming up in a roll with the ball in her hand. For a moment she was disorientated, finding herself facing away from the other players towards the boundary edge.

The wrong way. Turn around.

She spun, heaving the ball with all her might at the same time. It was a pretty poor throw, but it was in the general vicinity of the stumps, and for practically the first time in the game, Margaret managed to gather it. She twisted, breaking the stumps with the ball held in her large wicketkeeper's gloves, just as the opposition batsman dived.

A huge cheer went up from the Milton Road players. Madeline, still smarting from dropping the catch, could barely believe it as players came running over to her, patting her shoulder.

'Nice one,' Ruby said. 'That was epic. You sucked and ruled at the same time.'

As the players headed away, buzzing with excitement, back towards the changing rooms, Darren came over.

'That was brilliant,' he said. 'You won us the game. You've only played one game and you're already a club legend.'

Madeline just stared at him, nearly speechless.

'Uh?'

17

THE FACE OF THE ENEMY

'So, you're torn between your ex-boyfriend, who's starting hanging around again, and this new guy who's interested in you?' Janine gave a slow nod. 'Are you familiar with the seven deadly sins?'

'Ah, a little.'

'Greed. That's the keyword here. You are infected, Madeline, with a sense of greed. That you can have any man that you want. Maybe that was true at school, when you were bullying weaker girls who had bucked teeth, but in the adult world, it's an adjective that will ensure you fall into life's firepit. Is that want you really want? To burn in hell?'

'I ... ah....'

'Do you know how it feels to be that weaker child, the one mocked by its peers, forever in the shadow of more attractive, more popular people?'

'No, I—'

'Of course you don't. But time is a great leveler. So when one can look out of the window at one's Mercedes parked next to another's bicycle, to look at the picture of one's handsome, well-dressed and wealthy fiancé compared to another's singleness, it is easy to see the mastery of time at work, and all it took was a little nip-and-tuck, a little dental realignment … do you really understand?'

Madeline was about to make some noncommittal response when Janine tapped her watch. 'I'm afraid we're done for the day. We did some good work, I think. I'll see you next Tuesday.'

'I'm not sure this is working out—'

'Nonsense. I've seen a great change in you over the last two weeks, Madeline. You'd be a fool to drop out of the program now. Plus, ask Edith in reception about our loyalty discount.'

'But, what if—'

Janine put up a hand. 'If I answer any questions now, we'll be into overtime, which is the regular fee times five plus an administration fee. Are you happy to proceed?'

Madeline just flapped a hand and headed for the door.

'I'll see you next week,' Janine said, not looking up, instead pulling a smartphone out of her pocket and slouching back in her chair. Madeline caught a glimpse of a social media app before she went out.

The weather turned again at the beginning of the next week, rain lashing the windows of the café, the wind ripping the leaves off the trees as Madeline sat in Angela's easy chair with Hazel curled in her lap, drinking clotted cream lattes and reading the paperback books from a bring-and-share box she had set up inside the café's door. Ruby had an exam to prepare for so took the week off, but for several days practically the only people Madeline saw were Dan on his way home from work and Pete on his way to set up for the day, although with the weather his burger van had usually gone by midmorning.

Hazel was getting bigger by the day. Madeline had picked up a couple of cat towers from a garden centre out on the Brentwell to Willow River road, installing them into a couple of corners to give Hazel something to both scratch and climb. Local kids liked to stroke and feed her, so she had kept her food and water dishes by the front door, but had discretely hidden Hazel's litter tray in the back corridor that led to the upstairs flat. Where possible, though, Hazel preferred to go outside, and Madeline had contacted Angela about the possibility of putting in a cat flap in the wall beside the door, once Hazel was big enough to be safe from local strays.

Everything was going well, although time was drifting by. Each evening, however, as she came to lock up the café for the night, she couldn't help but stand by the door and look out at the park, wondering whether Rory would come striding out of the gloom.

'Is everything all right?' Jonas asked her, one rainy Wednesday night over dinner. 'You've been quiet for days. You know you can tell me, can't you?'

'Yes, Dad. Thanks.'

Normally, she would have spilled the beans, but where Rory was concerned, Jonas was unlikely to be sympathetic.

Sometimes they watched a bit of TV together after dinner, but Jonas had some stuff to do in the garage, and Madeline was in a lonesome mood, so she went up to her bedroom and got out her old laptop. Initially intending just to waste a little time, she found herself lingering over a couple of social media pages, itching to search for her former boyfriend.

Eventually she cracked, but to her surprise, Rory hadn't updated anything in years. It was as though he had gone off the grid, forgoing social media in a way that was rare among their shared generation. Instead, for a while Madeline wasted some time watching online videos, before deciding to go to bed. Just as she was about to switch off, however, she had a thought.

Rory might not be on the regular social pages, but he looked snappy in his suit and had told her he worked for a company. Perhaps he was on the business ones these days? Perhaps it was a company requirement that he maintain a certain social presence. Maybe his company forbade the posting of cat videos, holiday snaps, and memes.

She googled his name. The first page was all links to his inactive social media pages, but as she clicked onto page two of the search results, a new photo caught her eye, one she had not seen before. She clicked the link.

A picture of Rory as she knew him now appeared, all suave cool and smart business suit. Beneath his name on a short bio, it said, Managing Director. Below was some spiel about how Rory had changed the company around, turning it into the powerhouse it was today. He had clearly done well for himself, and Madeline found herself smiling. Sure, she had a bit of a hippy ethos about her, but she was still impressed by what he had achieved. Wondering what company he worked for, she clicked on a logo in the top corner.

Her heart skipped a beat.

Snide and Company Parking Contractors.

The company responsible for trying to privatise the theatre car park.

A cold sweat broke out across Madeline's back. Soon,

Sycamore Park's parking would no longer be free, vicious fines would be handed out to those who stayed too long or strayed over the lines of their spaces. Several bus tours had threatened to boycott the move, and the drop in custom could cause the theatre to close.

And it would all be Rory's fault.

18

CHANGES

'THIS IS A CAFÉ, NOT A LIBRARY,' Ruby said, clicking her fingers beside Madeline's face as she stood staring out of the open door across the park. 'Like, I'm not expecting you to start barn dancing or anything, but a bit of life wouldn't hurt.'

Madeline turned. 'Sorry, what?'

'Look, we've got no customers, so how about you come over here to the counter, sit down, and tell Auntie Ruby and Auntie Hazel all about your problems?'

Rubbing against Madeline's leg, Hazel meowed, as though to suggest this was a good idea.

'You can't tell anyone,' Madeline said.

'Not even the cricket team?'

'Of course not the cricket team!'

Ruby put up a hand. 'All right, all right. We'll keep your secrets between us, won't we, Hazel?'

The little cat meowed again.

Ruby made coffees. Hazel climbed up into a hanging basket at the top of a cat tower inside the door. Madeline considered what she could say.

'I've been getting closer to my ex,' she said, climbing onto a stool. 'He's been showing up from time to time, usually late in the evening.' Was that too much of an exaggeration? Twice. He had stopped by just twice. And nothing much had happened other than a brief chat about the past.

'Is that so?' Ruby said, nodding sagely, sounding wise beyond her years. 'You know to knock that on the head right now, don't you?'

'He's changed.'

Ruby leaned forward. 'People. Don't. Change.' She shrugged. 'Well, maybe clothes and hair colour. And if he was a clown before, he might not be acting like a clown now, but inside, he's still a clown.'

'That's a bit of a generalisation.'

'But it's true. Like, when I go out to bat for the club, I act like some angry nutjob, smashing the other team's bowlers all over the place, but the whole time I'm suppressing my inner nerd, refusing to allow myself to play the low risk shots, to just tap the ball into the gaps, the whole time while calculating what we need to win. Once the daughter of a mathematician, always the daughter of a mathematician.'

Madeline smiled. 'So, while on the outside you're Ruby, on the inside, you're still Rubik.'

Ruby closed her eyes. 'Please don't say that name. It burns. It burns every time.'

'I'm thinking of cutting my hair,' Madeline said. 'You know, shed the hippy look a bit. I kind of feel I've outgrown the braids a little. I might go for a neat bob or something.'

'I have a mate,' Ruby said. 'And while I agree, those things might be a little ungainly, you can't just hack them off. May I suggest a colourant?'

'I hadn't thought about it, but … maybe.'

'You have lovely fair hair. It'll take a dye so well.'

Madeline smiled. 'I'll think about it. Do you think Rory —' She stopped, shaking her head. 'Nothing.'

'Rory? That's his name?' Ruby's eyes narrowed. 'I think you should do the exact opposite of what you think he would like.'

'I told you, he's different now. He's more mature. He used to be kind of a free spirit, but he's … smartened up.'

Ruby sighed. 'It's your life.'

Madeline grimaced. 'There's one more thing—'

Rory's job was on the tip of her tongue, but at that moment the door opened and an older couple came in, bringing a terrier on a lead. It immediately starting barking at Hazel, who bolted up to the tower's highest platform and sat cowering just out of sight, tail wrapped protectively around her.

'Two lattes, please,' the lady said, struggling with the dog. 'But it might be quieter if we have them outside.'

Jonas let out a gasp as he came up the stairs in his slippers, carrying a cup of tea and a book. Madeline had left the bathroom door open, mostly to help get rid of the smell, and was staring at her new hair colour for the first time. Having used a local hairdresser to cut her hair into a tidy, shoulder-length bob, she had dyed it herself, and what had formerly been light brown was now a dark, rich auburn. Not quite as rebellious as Ruby's vibrant changes, but nevertheless she thought it looked pretty good.

'Wow. Is that really my daughter?'

'What do you think, Dad?'

Jonas smiled. 'I think it looks … nice.'

'Just nice?'

He rubbed the top of his head. 'Having little hair left, I'm pretty jealous. At least it's not purple.'

'That's next week.'

'I can't wait. Goodnight, love.'

'Night, Dad.'

As Jonas went into his room, Madeline turned back to the mirror. She looked about as different now as Rory did to the man she had been together with. He hadn't seemed much impressed with her braids, but maybe this new look would make him notice her … if he showed up again.

Only as she turned away from the mirror and switched off the bathroom light did she have a sudden pang of regret.

What I am doing? Did I really do this to impress my ex?

Ruby thought it was awesome. So did Dan and Pete. Hazel didn't appear to care, but Milady gave her a supportive bark.

Friday night, the fog had closed in again, and Sycamore Park was starting to shed its leaves. The trees were turning mottled shades of brown and orange, and around the bases of the trees the leaves were beginning to pile up. With the park's street lights glowing through the fog as leaves drifted down from the trees above, everything felt mystical and ancient. She thought about herds of deer racing through the forest, of druids chanting beside standing stones, of foxes standing up on their back legs to speak. With a smile, she started to close the door, then paused.

From the direction of the playground, a figure

appeared out of the fog. Wearing a suit and carrying a briefcase, he raised a hand.

Madeline's heart skipped a beat. She stood motionless in the doorway like a military wife watching her husband return from the front. As Rory reached her, it was all she could do not to throw herself into his arms.

'Thank God you're still open,' he said, coming to a stop. He wiped a hand across his hair, and a few dislodged strands of a gelled combover slipped back into place.

'I was just about to close,' Madeline said, unable to hide a smile. 'But for you I can stay open a few more minutes.'

He smiled, holding her gaze. 'I'll have a walnut latte please.'

She made the coffee while he set his briefcase down. He reached up to stroke Hazel, sitting at the top of the tower, but the little kitten hissed at him, so he hastily withdrew his hand.

'Sorry about that,' Madeline said. 'She's usually very friendly.'

Rory shrugged. 'Perhaps she's just tired.'

'She's a cat,' Madeline said. 'They can be temperamental.'

'Yes, this is true. So, how have you been?'

Madeline shrugged. 'Oh, you know, not bad. You?'

'Just busy. You know how it is. Climbing the corporate ladder, it's not just about making money. You have to put in the hard yards, secure the deals.'

Madeline suddenly remembered what he did for a living, and felt a pang of guilt, as though she was colluding with the enemy. Lots of regulars had mentioned the proposed privatisation of the car park, and not a single one had said anything positive. Perhaps ... hearing it direct from Rory might give her a better perspective.

'I … ah, I googled you,' she said, bringing over his drink and setting it down. 'I found out who you work for.'

Rory's eyes momentarily hardened, in that way they had when they were together, as a prelude to some tantrum which would involve a childish rant, the stamping of feet, sometimes the throwing of an object within close proximity. This time, though, he appeared to get a hold of himself, taking a deep breath, smoothing down his jacket.

'A job's a job,' he said, taking a sip of his coffee.

'It must be hard, you know, doing something like that.'

Rory turned in his seat. 'Because everyone thinks I'm some evil dictator, there to take away their freedom?'

'Well—'

'They don't understand,' he said. 'What my firm does is a good thing. We create more spaces. We regulate the car park so you don't have people leaving their car in the corner somewhere, walking up to the station, and going on holiday for two weeks. We prevent the abuse of a public service, and we feed money back into the community.'

'In what way?'

He paused a moment. 'In *many* ways.'

'For example?'

Rory's eyes narrowed. 'Last Christmas, we paid for the lights and the tree outside Brentwell Station. Did you see them?'

'I was in Australia.'

Rory shrugged. 'They were the best lights in the area.'

'That's … great.'

'You see? People want to demonise us, but we're doing good for the community.'

His chest was heaving for a fight. Madeline forced herself to smile. 'I'm sure it'll work out.'

'Yes,' Rory said. 'It will.'

They fell into an awkward period of small talk. Rory

was tense, like a rooster whose feathers had been ruffled, his pride hurt. Eventually, the talk came around to the café again, and this time, as Rory asked her about the number of seats they had, and what was popular on the menu, he pulled out a small notepad embossed with Snide and Company's logo, and began to make notes.

'Are you thinking about having a party here?' Madeline asked.

'Something like that. You would be prepared to stay open late, wouldn't you?'

'Within reason. I think the trading license is until nine o'clock.'

'That would work.'

'Do you have any specific date in mind?'

'November eleventh. It's a Saturday.'

'And how many people?'

Rory shrugged. 'Roughly fifty. I don't have specific numbers yet, but I'll let you know closer to the time.'

'Would you like to make a booking, then?'

He finished his coffee and stood up. 'Provisionally,' he said. 'I'll confirm at a later date.' Then, finally, he smiled. 'Thanks, Madeline. I knew I could count on you. So maybe people like to judge me these days, but you're the same old Madeline. I appreciate that.'

He slipped on his jacket and picked up his briefcase. As he headed for the door, he poked a finger towards Hazel who hissed again, then he was gone, walking off into the dark.

This time he didn't look back.

Madeline stood by the door for a long time. Hazel climbed down from the cat tower and rubbed her leg, offering moral support. So much to digest, so much to unpack. *The same old Madeline.* That had cut deep. That he hadn't mentioned her hair, that had hurt too. That he had looked on the verge of a familiar tantrum before getting hold of himself, another black mark.

Perhaps he wasn't the Rory she remembered, after all. Perhaps this version was even worse.

She closed the door and went back inside, flipping over the CLOSED sign. The wind had got up, rattling against the windows. Hazel jumped up into her arms, purring loudly, a little vibrating machine.

'You didn't like him, did you?' Madeline said to the little cat as she stroked Hazel's head. 'I'm starting to think that I don't like him either.'

PET TALES

'I CAN'T BELIEVE IT,' Jonas said, throwing the piece of paper down on the table. 'Those utter toads. A hundred and seventy-five quid for not parking in my allocated space. Look at this.' He held up a printed photograph taken from the rear of a car, showing the wheels lined up along a white line. 'I'm half an inch over. That's it. A hundred and seventy-five quid. If they hadn't redrawn the lights six inches narrower, there wouldn't have been a problem.'

'Do you want a drink, Dad?'

'I want to get hold of whoever runs Snide and Company and rip out their throat. This is going to Trading Standards.' He scooped up the letter again and began rifling through drawers, looking for envelopes and writing paper.

Madeline said nothing. How could she tell him what she knew? Part of her agreed with her dad, but there was still that little part of her that wouldn't let go, that wanted to believe Rory, to continue seeing him as a new, improved version of the man she had once loved, even if all the evidence pointed to the contrary.

'You know, I tried to call them,' Jonas said, not looking up. 'But there's no number on their website. What kind of a useless company doesn't have a customer services hotline? Although I bet if they did, it would all be automated. Honestly, this country should be ashamed of itself, letting companies like this get a foot in the door.'

Madeline just nodded. Perhaps next time she saw Rory, she could have a word?

Jonas was still ranting. 'Your brother said I should just show up at the head office and complain, but of course, there's no company address listed either.' He looked up and gave her a tired smile. 'Amy suggested I get a bicycle.'

'Maybe we all should,' Madeline said. 'Shall I get you a glass of wine?'

Monday was one of Ruby's days off, but the air was filled with drizzly showers so the park was deserted all day. Pete stopped in for a coffee and a chat, before announcing he was going home early, but Madeline decided to hang on in case there was a rush of customers over lunchtime. However, the only person who stopped in was Lizzie from the library next door, who stopped for just a five-minute chat before leaving with a takeaway espresso and a slice of cake, so Madeline pulled Angela's easy chair out from the kitchen and put it near the window, reading a book while Hazel slept in her lap.

At just after four o'clock, she was about ready to close when she caught sight of a man walking up from the playground in the direction of the café.

Often customers would approach close enough to read the specials board outside or check the opening times, before veering off towards the library and the theatre or out to the main north gates, but a moment after he went out of sight behind the window frame, the tinkle of the bell above the door sounded, and Madeline heard shoes wiping on the mat. She lifted Hazel off her lap so she could get up, replacing the cat on the warm part of the chair.

'Hello?'

Madeline walked back through the tables until the man came into sight. 'Oh, hello.'

Darren Smith flinched with surprise, a smile breaking out across his face. 'I'm sorry, I didn't recognise you at first. Wow, your hair looks amazing. I don't mean to say that it looked bad before, just that I really like what you've done with it. It's very … seasonal.'

Despite her best efforts, Madeline found herself blushing. 'Uh, thanks. Can I get you something?'

'Sure. Coffee would be great. Just normal is fine, without all the bells and whistles. Can I … ah … get you one, too? You don't look too busy.'

Madeline shrugged. 'Just me and the cat.'

Darren glanced past her at Hazel sitting on the chair. 'She's getting big.'

Madeline smiled. 'They grow up quick, don't they?'

Darren smiled. 'So, how have you been?'

'You mean, since the cricket match?'

'You know, life in general.'

'Oh, not too bad.'

'That's good.'

'And you?'

'Yeah, the usual. Mondays are a day off. I just thought I'd stop by, and you know, say hello.'

'You came here just to see me?'

It was Darren's turn to blush, meaning Madeline knew the answer, no matter what he said. 'Um, yeah. And the cat, of course. I wanted to see if you were free for a cricket match on Sunday.'

'A cricket match?'

'Yeah. The final was supposed to be last week, but it got cancelled due to rain. It's been moved to next Sunday, but we have three regular guys unavailable. League rules mean we need at least eight players. So far, we have seven.'

'Ah, I don't know.'

'Go on,' Darren said with another smile. 'If you like, I can come by and give you a bit of practice after work. We could throw a tennis ball around in the park.'

If this was Darren's idea of a date, it was the most unique yet simple one Madeline had ever heard. She opened her mouth to say yes, then thought of Rory. What would he think if he found her playing cricket with Darren? What would he ... *why would it matter?*

'Is that a no?'

'Sorry?'

'You were kind of shaking your head.'

'No, I mean, not no, I'm just....' She looked up and shrugged. 'I'm just scared.'

'We can use a tennis ball, or perhaps a sponge ball, if that helps. Maybe a ping pong ball?'

Madeline grinned. 'What kind of a coward do you think I am?'

'Sorry, I didn't mean—'

'I'm joking. Like, look at me, I'm a comedian. I mean, sorry ... just ... yeah.'

Madeline wished her heart would stop fluttering and allow her to get hold of her senses. The words were jumbling over themselves, making her say the stupidest things.

'Why don't we have that coffee?'

Madeline nodded, then tapped a hand on the

countertop as though she was an escaped mental patient. 'Yeah. That's a plan, isn't it?'

She fled to the kitchen, burying her head. Out in the café, she heard Darren muttering sweet things to Hazel.

Don't say anything stupid. He clearly likes you. And he's nice. He's really nice.

(Rory Rory Rory)

Rory threw my cake away. Rory didn't notice my hair. Rory works for a scumbag private company who just fined my dad for parking one inch over the white lines.

She slammed a fist down on the countertop, hard enough to make the pots and pans in the overhead cupboard rattle.

'Are you all right in there?'

Madeline shook her head. 'Yes, yes, I'm fine.'

She had turned off the machines but was able to focus long enough to make two instant coffees and carry them out to the shop without spilling them. Setting them down, she moved a safe distance away, aware that a flapping hand might knock them over.

Darren was standing by the window, cradling a purring Hazel in his arms.

'Such a sweet little thing,' he said, turning to Madeline. 'You did a great job saving her. I wish we could save them all, but sadly life doesn't work that way.'

'It must make a change to have an animal that likes you,' Madeline said.

Darren grinned. 'For sure. You have no idea how many times I've been snarled at, scratched and bitten.'

'Do you have any pets of your own?'

Darren shook his head. 'No. I don't really have the time. I mean, I'd like a dog one day, one I could walk in the park, but it's hard when you deal with sick animals all day long. I see the looks in the faces of the customers when I have to tell them that their pet isn't coming back, and I dread the idea of it being me.'

'Did you always want to be a vet?'

Darren set Hazel down on the floor and took a stool at the counter. 'I had a little dog when I was young,' he said. 'A beagle. His name was Jim.' He smiled. 'I loved that little thing so much. We went everywhere together, and he used to wait for me when I got home from school every day. One day, though, when I was thirteen or fourteen, he wasn't there. He'd got sick. He was only seven or eight years old, but there was nothing the vet could do. He had a form of cancer. It broke my heart, but the day that Jim died, I promised myself I would become a vet, and do everything I could to stop other kids like me having to see their pets die so young.'

Madeline had reached for his hand without realising it. Now, seeing her fingers hovering just inches above his, she jerked her hand away.

'That's so … sad,' she said. 'But nice at the same time.'

'What about you? Did you have a lot of pets when you were a kid?'

'I had a rabbit,' Madeline said with a smile. 'Her name was Mrs. Bunce. One day my idiot little brother forgot to lock the cage and next door's cat got her.'

'Ah, that's too bad.'

Madeline shrugged. 'I was heartbroken for about a week, but then my parents got me a hamster, so I got over it.' She smiled. 'I've always wanted a dog or something too, but I've been living abroad for the last eight years, so it's not been possible. A few of the people I worked for had pets, so that was enough.'

'What were you doing overseas?'

'Oh, this and that. I moved about every year or so. I did some teaching, a bit of nannying.'

'I'd love to hear all about it. I've only ever been to France.'

'Really?'

'On the ferry from Plymouth.'

'You've never been on an aeroplane?'

Darren shrugged. 'I went to Scotland once on one of those little local flights. I wasn't impressed. I got the train back.'

'Really?'

'Yeah, it's not that I was scared or anything, it's just there wasn't any food, and it was so packed you couldn't see anything. On the train I got a nice first-class seat, enjoyed decent food, and looked out of the window for twelve hours.'

'Twelve?'

'Yeah, it took a while, I have to say.'

'You went first-class?'

Darren gave a sheepish shrug. 'I'm a vet,' he said. 'It pays all right. And I don't get out much.'

'The big airlines are totally different to those little hopper things,' Madeline said. 'They actually feed you, and they're relatively comfortable. Some are better than others, though.'

'Maybe one day. So, I gather you're not here long. That you're going to go overseas again at some point?'

Madeline felt a pang of regret. 'Probably. I've never really felt settled here. When I'm travelling, I kind of feel like I'm in the right place, even if that place is changing all the time.'

'Yeah?'

'Maybe I'm trying to find my place in the world, something like that. I don't know. I just never really feel settled anywhere. Although, being back here, working at this café, it's been different to what I expected. Initially my aim was just to save enough money to go back overseas, but the longer I'm here, the more I like it. The cold air in the mornings, even the fog … it's weird, but I find it kind of comforting. And when you get regular customers come in, I kind of see them like old friends. There are people that come in at the same time every week, and if they don't come … I miss them. Is that weird?'

'Maybe you're starting to find what you've been looking for.'

The coffee got cold. Before Madeline realised, it was nearly six o'clock, and they'd been talking in front of two cold coffees for nearly two hours. The initial nerves had gone, and she found herself talking to Darren like an old friend, telling him her hopes and fears, her dreams, her insecurities, and the whole time he listened intently, eyes never leaving hers, as though there was no place in the world he would rather be.

It was Hazel who broke the spell, meowing at the door to be let out. Darren looked up at the clock on the wall. His eyes widened and he gave Madeline a sheepish grin.

'Wow, sorry for taking up so much of your time,' he said.

'No, no, it's fine,' Madeline said, jumping up to open the door and let Hazel outside. She stayed by the door, keeping an eye on the little cat as she wandered across the path to the trees and the leaves fallen around them, where she began to jump and pounce as though each leaf were a mouse needing to be caught.

'I mean it, I'm really sorry. It's getting late, and you probably need to get home for dinner.'

'You do, too, I imagine.'

Darren shrugged and grinned. 'There'll be something in the freezer. Unless … you wanted to get something?'

Madeline's heart screamed at her to say yes, but by now Dad would have cooked, and she didn't want to disappoint him. He laid out the table at seven every day unless she told him she was going out.

'I can't,' she said. 'My dad will have cooked.'

'That's okay. Another time. How about Wednesday? The clinic stays open late on Tuesdays, but Wednesday I finish early. Any time after five is fine. Perhaps we could throw a ball for half an hour first?' He grinned. 'Work up an appetite.'

(Rory Rory Rory)

(Hazel hates him)

Madeline smiled, and a plume of heat flushed through her. 'That would be great,' she said. 'Ruby works Wednesday, but we're never that busy in the afternoons, so I can probably finish at five and leave Ruby to close up.'

'It's a date.'

(Oh my god, it's a date)

Madeline's throat felt a millimetre wide as she croaked, 'Yes.'

'See you then.'

'Yes.'

Darren went out. As he walked across the path, Hazel pounced on his shoe, as though to stop him leaving. He reached down, gave the little cat a stroke, flashed a smile at Madeline, and went on his way.

She leaned against the door frame and watched him go, feeling all gooey inside like a warm, melting marshmallow.

Before he disappeared around the path as it wound out of sight towards the playground, he looked back and waved, not once, but twice.

20

REVELATIONS

JANINE LEANED FORWARDS, a sour look on her face, and not for the first time today, Madeline wished she'd just trusted her own thoughts and not shown up.

'So, let me get this straight. You've found yourself attracted to your ex-boyfriend, and now someone else has come along. And you feel torn between the two?'

'Something like that.'

Janine shook her head. 'I think what we need to do here is not so much heal you, as cure you. Don't you find your behaviour despicable?'

'Excuse me?'

'Carrying on with two men at the same time?'

'I'm not actually carrying on with either of them. One has been randomly showing up, and the other just asked me for a date.'

'And you said yes?'

Madeline nodded. 'And now I feel guilty.'

'I should think so. What if your ex-boyfriend, burned by the experience of being with you in the past, has been building up to asking you out, laying the groundwork, and now at the drop of a rather filthy hat, you've pulled the rug out from under him? Don't you feel ashamed?'

'I haven't pulled the rug out from under anyone. And aren't you supposed to be helping me with this?'

'Some people are beyond help. I think you should grovel at your ex-boyfriend's feet and beg for forgiveness. After all, if he put up with your wanton decisions before and he's still interested, he must be worth his weight in gold.'

'That's just it. I'm not sure if he is still interested. He threw my chocolate cake in the duck pond, didn't even notice that I completely changed my hair, and my cat hates him.'

'I would be hard pushed to find someone as petty as you.'

Madeline frowned. 'Really?'

'I'd like to say you disgust me, but I'm not allowed to use such language with my clients. It undermines their confidence. However, I will say that you disappoint me. I mean, I know you were a shallow bully at school, but I thought you might have matured just a little bit since then. It does seem, however, that I might have to make the rare decision to admit I was wrong.' Janine shifted in her seat, adjusting her perfectly tailored suit, and stood up. 'Please excuse me for a moment. I have to go to the bathroom. And it's not to be sick, as you might think, having had to listen to your pathetic excuses for problems for the last half an hour, but simply to take care of regular bodily functions.'

'Okay.'

As Janine went out, Madeline leaned back in the chair, wondering how much longer she could handle this exercise in self-flagellation. She had told Ruby about her last session with Janine. Ruby had cried with laughter and told

Madeline she should record it, set it to music, and put it on TikTok. Today, though, Janine was in imperious form.

Needing to stretch her legs, Madeline got up, and wandered past Janine's desk to the window. She could just see the theatre. Ruby had suggested they take in a show sometime, as there was a hip-hop version of Wizard of Oz opening in a couple of weeks. Madeline had been more interested in a travelling performance of Cats, but Ruby had rolled her eyes and told her to modernise.

The door opened, and Madeline spun around. Janine came back in, but just before Madeline hurried to sit down, her eyes scanned Janine's desktop. Behind the rack of files which hid most of it from a client's view were a handful of knickknacks from overseas trips—a metal Eiffel Tower, a paperweight with the Sydney Opera house inside, a line of Matryoshka dolls. And there was a little laptop, one of the micro-sized ones that could practically slip into a back pocket, barely bigger than a phone. It was open, a photo collage screensaver constantly shifting.

And Madeline found herself transfixed by images of Janine and Rory in a multitude of romantic poses, arms around each other, lips pressed to cheeks, hands held, engagement rings gleaming.

In a trance, she stumbled back to her seat.

Janine marched back behind her desk and sat down. She lifted a pocket watch, peered at it, and said, 'I think we've gone overtime. I'll ask Edith to adjust today's fee. We did some good work today, Madeline. I see a ray of light for you. It's not too late. I'll see you next week. In the meantime, I would suggest attempting to focus on your work, and keep your roving mind out of trouble.'

Madeline just stared at her. 'Okay,' was all she could bring herself to say.

Ruby was in combative mood. 'So what's he doing showing up here if he's engaged to that therapist troll?' she said. 'Honestly, the only good thing about you going there is that you now know the truth. I hope you cancelled next week's session?'

Madeline grimaced. 'You know when you have a bruise and you keep pressing it, even though it totally hurts?'

'You're not going again?'

'Well, I might, you know, just once more. You see, I'm armed with information that I didn't have before.'

'That this ex-boyfriend she keeps berating you for liking is actually her own current boyfriend?'

'Something like that.'

'But you know that on that score, I agree with her. He's a scumbag. You should kick him out to roost, or whatever you old people say. Block him on Snapchat.'

'What would you do?'

'You know what I did to some guy who bullied me at school?'

'Do I want to know?'

'I found out he hated rats. So I put one in his school locker.'

'A real rat?'

Ruby rolled her eyes. 'No, of course not a real rat. It like was a toy one. But I hung a little sign around its neck that said, "Mess with me, you mess with my whole extended family." That told him.'

'Did he understand?'

Ruby shrugged. 'I'm not sure. I'm an only child, so he probably didn't know it was me. But it spooked him, you know.'

'That's all?'

'My dad was his maths teacher. I tried to convince him to give this kid a low test score, but Dad said that wasn't ethical. He did promise to glare at him from time to time.'

Madeline smiled. 'It's great when your parents have your back. My dad hates Rory. He'd go mental if he knew I was talking to him again.'

'You have to call him out on this next time he shows up. You can't have him playing you for a mug. Promise me?' Ruby held up her fingers in a weird fork shape.

'What's that?'

'Secret code for yes. I made a new version, because no one takes the old versions seriously anymore.'

'Oh, okay.'

'Touch it.'

Madeline pressed her fingers against Ruby's. 'Promise.'

'You have to touch all three in a kind of piano motion, one at a time.'

'Seriously?'

'Yes. Just do it.'

'I promise.'

'No, you have to say "I promise" as you roll your fingers across mine.'

'Can't we do something easier?'

'No, because this seals it. You have to call him out. If you don't ... well, that's something you'll have to live with.'

'Got it.'

'Good.'

Wednesday was a little overcast but still warm, so the café was fairly busy, all the dog walkers and couples coming in for afternoon coffee. Madeline was on edge as her date with Darren approached, and Ruby delighted in winding her up about it, at one point even taking down the clock above the counter and winding it forwards two hours while Madeline was in the kitchen, throwing her into a sudden panic when she saw it showing ten to five.

'Just … relax.'

'I'm trying to. It's not easy. I haven't been on a date in years.'

'Look, if it makes you feel better, he's nervous as hell. He texted me last night to ask what colours you like. I think he was selecting his clothes or something.'

'What did you tell him?'

'I said you're a sucker for lemon yellow and lime green, and that you really like luminous headbands.'

'Seriously?'

Ruby rolled her eyes. 'No, of course not. I told him to stop being such a tool and wear whatever he liked.'

'Thank god for that.'

'And that as long as he remembered the headband, he was all good.'

Madeline just shook her head. 'Well, I suppose I should be happy if he shows up.'

'He will. Barring a car crash or a sudden onset of mad cow disease, he'll be here.'

'Do you think I look okay?'

'You look pretty much the same as you did all of last week, so I imagine you'll be fine.'

'I can't believe I'm asking for dating advice from a student.'

Ruby grinned. 'Neither can I.'

As five o'clock approached, the customers began to leave. By five to five, only Madeline and Ruby were left. Ruby still had her apron on, but Madeline had taken hers off, ready for Darren's arrival. As the door opened, however, Hazel's hiss told her something was wrong.

'Oh, hi,' Rory said, smiling at Ruby. 'You must be the part time girl. Becky, wasn't it?'

'Ruby,' Ruby said. 'We're closed.'

Rory looked at his watch. 'It's a bit early for that, isn't it? Sorry, I won't keep you. I just wanted a word with Madeline here.'

Madeline was sweating, heart palpitating, throat seizing up. Unable to speak properly, she pulled Ruby aside.

'Go … outside,' she croaked into Ruby's ear. 'Keep Darren away. I'll get rid of him as quick as I can.'

'There's just something I'd like to talk about,' Rory said, putting his briefcase down on a tabletop. 'It'll only take ten minutes.'

Through the window, to her horror Madeline saw Darren walking up the path from the playground. He paused briefly in the mosaic plaza to admire Big Gerry, the park's largest sycamore, then turned heading for the café.

'Go!' Madeline hissed at Ruby.

Ruby hurried to the door, scooping up Hazel and tucking her under her arm. Madeline, not wanting to see Darren through the window, pulled up a chair facing away. Rory, perhaps sensing that was the last thing she wanted him to do, reached out and gave her shoulder a touch that once might have been affectionate.

'We're about to close,' Madeline said. 'What is it you're after?'

Rory sat down. Madeline realised her mistake, because he was facing the window. Every few seconds he would glance up at the window and smile. Madeline, dying inside, didn't dare turn around.

'This is a little hard for me to say,' Rory said, pulling a

clear plastic file out of his bag and laying it on the table. 'I mean, I know we have history and everything, and I really hoped to find somewhere else, but this place is just perfect.' He looked around the inside of the café as though he'd never seen it before. 'Quaint, rustic … *romantic*. It's the perfect place to get married.'

She glanced down at his finger and saw the ring shining there. It had never been there before, because she had checked, but now it sparkled at her. She could almost hear the horrid little circle of metal laughing.

I hope it turns you into a troll.

'I didn't know how to tell you at first,' Rory said. 'Because I knew it would hurt you. I could tell you still had a flame for me, and to be honest, I've never really extinguished mine for you.'

Please shut up. Please shut up right now.

'And, well, my fiancée, you'll know her, which might make it worse, like rubbing sand into the wound. Janine Woodfield? You remember her from school?'

I wish Hazel would suddenly transform into a lion and eat you.

'Well, she's changed a lot—I mean, she was a bit of a dog before, wasn't she? Amazing how money and a little time on the surgeon's table can sort you out, isn't it? And I've changed, too. And I guess life just pushed us together.'

Your stupid company fined my dad for going one inch over the white line.

'So anyway, I hope I didn't lead you on or anything. I mean, when I'm near you, I find it hard not to just slip into the old routine, but I have to remember times have changed. You're older now, you're not the same girl I knew eight years ago. Even if you do look more or less the same.'

More or less. Destroy him.

'So, what I'm asking is for Janine and me to have our wedding here. We'll provide everything, all you need to do is provide the space and the food. We can talk about the menu at a later date. Honestly, it'll be great. As you've probably noticed, both Janine and I are pretty well off these days, so we're offering a fee far higher than a café like this usually makes at this time of year. Plus, I've invited a whole bunch of people from school, so there should be several people you know. Won't that be great? I managed to track down several of your old cross-country team. It won't just be a wedding, it'll be a school reunion at the same time.'

And an exercise in total humiliation.

'So, what do you say?'

She had to say something. She opened her mouth, trying to find sound.

'Uh.'

Rory grinned, then reached across the table and patted Madeline's hand. 'Brilliant. I knew you'd be cool with this. Honestly, it's been so great seeing you again, Madeline. I'm so glad you're back in town.'

'Uh?'

He slipped his clear plastic file back into his briefcase without ever actually showing it to her, then stood up.

'I'll be in touch again soon.' He patted her on the shoulder again, then walked past, moving through the tables. A few seconds later, Madeline heard the bell above the door tinkle. Even then, it was a few seconds before she could bring herself to turn around. When she did, she found Ruby standing in the open doorway, Hazel perched on her shoulder. Both looked sad.

'Darren?' she croaked.

Ruby shook her head. 'He's gone,' she said.

21

BREAKING AND REBUILDING

As though to amplify Madeline's mood, it bucketed with rain for the next week. The cricket final was cancelled. According to Ruby, both captains wanted to play the game at some point, but a date was yet to be set, and with the year deep into October, it was unlikely that a suitable time could be found before the morning dew and the showers forced the cup to be shared.

The café stayed quiet, a handful of customers breaking up each day. Ruby came late and left early. And despite her assurances that Darren was fine with everything but just busy—'A lot of pets die in autumn,' Ruby claimed— Madeline neither saw nor heard from him. As she flipped the sign around to CLOSED and headed for what she planned to be her last session with Janine, she could barely stand up for the misery that hung like lead weights around her shoulders. At least Hazel seemed content, giving her a quick leg rub before jumping up onto the window ledge to scan for animals playing out in the rain.

Janine was in buoyant mood, waving Madeline to her seat with an extravagant flourish of her hands.

'I can just tell things are going well,' she said as she took her place behind her desk. 'You look like a different woman today. Did you change your glasses?'

Madeline shook her head. 'No.'

'Your hair?'

'No.'

Janine leaned forwards, her voice lowering as she said, 'Then it must be your attitude.'

'My ex-boyfriend is your fiancé,' Madeline said. 'You're having your wedding at my café on November eleventh.'

For the briefest of moments, Janine looked thrown. Then she settled back into her chair, brushed an imaginary piece of lint off her suit jacket, and said, 'It's impressive that you've come so far that such a situation is like water off a duck's back.'

'It's just business. This is the low season, so for a café like mine, it makes financial sense.'

'Financial sense,' Janine echoed. 'I'm so proud of you. Throwing your emotions into the gutter in order that you can move forwards. We've achieved so much together.'

Madeline stared at her, then forced the smile she had rehearsed in the mirror perhaps fifty times. 'I hope you and Rory are very happy together,' she said. 'I will make sure everything goes perfectly for you on your big day.'

Janine gave a slow nod. 'You've matured, too. It's beautiful.'

Madeline cleared her throat and stood up. 'Thank you for your time, Dr. Woodfield,' she said. 'I think I can move forwards on my own now.'

Janine smiled. Then, continuing to surprise Madeline, she began to clap. 'You're a revelation,' she said. 'Just a beautiful human being.'

Madeline could only force another smile and head for the door. In the reception she paid Edith on autopilot, then made her way outside. The moment the doors closed behind her, she let out a breath she felt she had been holding for days. She leaned forwards onto her knees, gasping for air.

Then, as soon as she had a hold of herself, she pulled out her phone and called Ruby.

'Yeah? You suddenly got busy and need me to come in?'

'I need a drinking partner,' Madeline said.

There was a pause. Then: 'Just let me finish typing this paragraph and I'm there.'

'Look, you're a grown woman. There's no way we should be doing this.'

'Film it and put it on Facebook,' Madeline slurred, as she peered through steamed up glasses at the river.

'What is this, 2012?' Ruby moaned. 'I'll put it on TikTok. I don't really think you want me to, though.'

'Come on. It's time to leap into the unknown. Achieve the impossible.'

'But there's a footbridge just over there.'

Redfield Canal, as far as Madeline could tell, was a raging torrent, swollen by the recent rain, water sloshing up over the bank. And the other side, only about fifteen feet—just wide enough in this section for two longboats to pass side by side—looked about a mile away.

'Look, it's probably only waist deep, but it'll still be filled with gunk, and you could land on something nasty, like a shopping trolly,' Ruby said. 'I really think you should reconsider this.'

Madeline, halfway up the bank, drunk on at least one bottle of wine—or was it two?—dug her feet into the turf.

'I have to prove myself,' she said. 'My whole life has been a meandering lie.'

'No, it really hasn't,' Ruby said.

'I have to do this.'

'No, you really don't. What you have to do is let me take you home, bang a couple of aspirin and then sleep it off. You know there's another bus tour due tomorrow, right?'

'One of the last,' Madeline said. 'Before the gates close on freedom forever.'

'So let's do something about it.'

'I can't. I need to jump across the canal.'

Ruby shrugged. 'All right, then. Good luck. I'm filming.'

Madeline took a deep breath. *All my life's failings can be resolved by jumping over the canal. It is the pinnacle of human achievement. The greatest of all things.*

She took a couple of steps forwards, then stopped at the edge of the bank. Water sloshed over her shoes. Her shoulders slumped. She turned to face Ruby.

'I want to go home,' she said.

Ruby sighed and lowered her phone. 'That was lame,' she said. 'All you needed to do was fall in, and we'd have had a million views in the can at least.'

Madeline woke up to find she had forgotten to close her curtains, and a bright sun was shining down on her bed. Her alarm clock read seven-thirty.

Only when she sat up did the headache hit her, along with flashes of memory from the night before. Her and Ruby drinking wine in the café until it was nearly nine o'clock, with rain battering the windows outside. Her snap decision to try to outdo Rory by jumping across the canal, something which had not only been extremely stupid, but impossible, now that she thought about it. She had no idea what the world long jump record was, but it couldn't be much more than the width of the canal, and the sloping bank, plus the short run up due to the fenced path at the top made it nearly impossible to get any momentum.

She suddenly had a flush of worry that she had forgotten to lock or even close the café's front door. She climbed out of bed, quickly got herself ready, then hurried out, stopping only briefly in the kitchen to swallow a couple more painkillers.

To her relief, the café was locked up tight, and Hazel greeted her as usual with a leg rub, before wanting to go outside. With one eye on the little cat as it chased falling leaves among the trees, Madeline wandered down to Pete's van for a coffee.

'Top of the morning to you,' Pete greeted her. 'You look like hell.'

'A night on the sauce,' Madeline told him. 'I had to exorcise a few demons.'

'We've all been there,' Pete said with a grin. 'Did you manage it?'

Madeline lifted a fist. 'I think so. I'll know better when the hangover passes, though.'

'Just let me know if you want it extra black,' Pete said. 'I've got a few dregs left over from yesterday.'

'I'll probably be good with the fresh,' Madeline said. 'But I'll keep it in mind. You've heard about the car park plans, haven't you?'

Pete's smile dropped. 'Can't be a good thing, can it? Picked up a fine myself from the same scumbag company a couple of months back. Put my details in the machine, paid up, no ticket came out. Next thing I know I have a demand for a hundred and twenty quid through the post and no way to dispute it. Someone needs to dig a big hole, chuck private parking companies in it, and concrete over the top.'

'Do you think there's anything we can do about it?'

Pete shrugged. 'No idea. I'd be happy to sign a petition, if there was one going around. And do you know Tom, the park caretaker? He's friends with Regina Clover, the local councillor. You could get him to have a word. I know Dan talks to him, so I'll give him a shout if I see him. You know what these council types are like, though. They won't do anything unless there's a profit in it for them.'

'But selling off the car park to Snide and Company won't benefit anyone,' Madeline said. 'Except Ev—the bosses at Snide.'

'That's the way these things work,' Pete said. 'Good luck with your campaigning, though. We're all right behind you.'

'Thanks.'

Madeline picked Hazel off a tree branch she had managed to climb up to and headed back to the café, mind heavy with ideas. A cool wind was blowing through the park, and it was still an hour away from the usual opening time, so she got herself a coffee and a slice of pie, grabbed a pen and a pad of paper and sat outside, leaves blowing around her as she jotted down ideas.

No one—literally no one—she had spoken to was in favour of the car park, and it sounded like Snide and Company's business practices were far from ethical. If she could get enough opposition to the car park, plus demonstrate Snide and Company's shady business model, perhaps the council would listen. Happy to have found a purpose, she got to work, drafting up a hand-written petition explaining her concerns about the car park's privatisation.

It was Tuesday, one of Ruby's days off, so Madeline flipped the sign to CLOSED and went up to the High Street, where she photocopied her petition in a printing shop and bought a couple of packs of notebooks to collect signatures.

On the way back, she dropped a few in at local shops on the way, explaining the situation to each shop owner. All of them were happy to help, putting her petition on their countertops.

Returning to the café, she put her petition by the door, then got to work with usual café business, preparing cakes and pies, checking stock, filling out order forms, making calls to suppliers. For the first time in a week she felt a real spring in her step.

The wind eased and the sun brought mid-October warmth. By mid-afternoon the café alone had collected twenty signatures for the petition, and Madeline was starting to feel like she might be able to make a real difference. As the afternoon rush eased, though, she started thinking about closing early, in order to drop her petition in at a few more places. She had already given copies to the library and the staff in the theatre's box office, while Pete had taken a couple of sheets for his customers. There were plenty of other businesses she hadn't been to yet, however, so after making sure Hazel was fed and her litter box changed, she closed the café just after three o'clock and headed out.

She went to the fish'n'chips shop, Brentwell Art Supplies, a couple of other cafés, even dropping one in at Evans Carpets, where a young man with an impressive mullet had been happy to take a couple of sheets. Eventually, however, she found herself standing outside the vets where Darren worked, trying to kid herself that this hadn't been her destination all along.

It wasn't busy. An old woman sat with a poodle in a carry cage in an otherwise empty waiting room. Madeline took a seat, a pile of notebooks and notices on her lap in lieu of any pets.

The woman was called into the consultation room. A few minutes later she came back out, looking a little happier than before. Madeline was alone.

The receptionist, not Ruby's friend Caroline today but an older lady with her grey hair tied back in a bun, asked if she needed help. Madeline, heart racing, asked to speak to Darren. The receptionist went back through a door, and a few seconds later the door to a consultation room opened and Darren, mask pulled down around his neck, leaned out.

'You can come in,' he said.

There was an awkward silence as the large consultation door slid closed behind them. Darren stood on one side of a large table on which pets were usually placed, Madeline on the other. Cabinets filled with medicines and equipment lined one wall. On the other was an advertisement for a new pet food formula.

'Hello,' Madeline said.

'Hello,' Darren replied, offering a little smile.

'Sorry about last week,' Madeline said, looking down. 'I should give you an explanation.'

Darren shook his head. 'Really, there's no need. You were busy. It's okay.'

'You're too forgiving. I effectively stood you up. You see, my ex-boyfriend showed up at exactly the wrong moment. Like, if I was writing that into a film script, I couldn't have done it better. And I'll admit, for a while I had a bit of a pining for him, you know? We were together a few years, but it kind of ended when I went overseas. We weren't suited then, but after a few years pass, your memory kind of glosses over the cracks. You forget all the stuff you didn't like, even if that was kind of the majority. And you amplify the good times.'

Darren smiled. 'Like when you're at university and all you remember is the parties and the crazy stuff, and you forget about the hours of sitting in the library staring at small lines of text and wishing you had the power to memorise it all?'

'Yeah, that would do it. So, I'll admit I was kind of torn for a while. But the reason he was there, believe it or not, was because he wants to hold his wedding at the Oak Leaf Café. I know that's kind of awkward, particularly as he just happens to be getting married to a woman who was in my class at school, and claims that I bullied her, but you know, it's just business. The café could probably do with a boost in revenue around this time of year.'

'That's completely understandable,' Darren said.

'However, I'm thinking of pulling the plug on it anyway,' Madeline said. 'You see, I found out something else about my ex-boyfriend. He's sold his soul to the devil.'

'He's a tax accountant?'

Madeline shook her head. 'Worse. Possibly. He's the managing director of a private parking company which is trying to buy the free council car park outside Brentwell Theatre.'

Darren smiled and gave a dramatic sigh. 'Truly the devil in another name. They approached me about buying my clinic's car park. They insisted they could get twelve spaces where there are currently eight, and told me I'd get thirty percent of any fines collected. I told them to take a hike.'

'I can't let it happen. So, if you'd be so kind, I'd really

like it if you could put a petition up in your clinic, and a notebook for people to sign.'

Darren nodded. 'Absolutely. I'll sign it first, get the ball rolling. And if there's anything else you'd like, just ask.'

Madeline felt her cheeks beginning to warm. Her brow felt damp, her heart thumping in her mouth.

'And … if you found yourself with nothing much to do, one afternoon, I'd really like it if you could stop by the café. I … have a few pie recipes I've been trying out, and I'd like a, um, a guinea pig to test them on. Plus, we're not so busy at this time of year, so a little company would be kind of nice.'

Darren looked down. When he looked up, he gave her a smile that cut through all her nerves, wrapping itself like a blanket around her heart.

'You know,' he said, 'it's getting a little colder, and I was thinking I ought to put on a little weight to keep myself warm. I think that would be a very good idea indeed. What time do you shut tonight?'

Madeline's mouth felt dry. 'Ah … sometime after you arrive?'

'Perfect. I'll see you then.'

22

A CHANGE IN THE WEATHER

SHE FRETTED ALL AFTERNOON, struggling to concentrate. The rain held off but clouds rolled in to blanket the sky, so the park and the café were quieter than usual. With no customers after four o'clock, Madeline grabbed a rake and a broom and went out to clear leaves off the path, piling them up beneath the trees, while Hazel made a nuisance of herself, dancing among the fluttering leaves, trying to bat them out of existence.

Tom, the burly caretaker who Pete had told her also acted in some of the theatre's productions, wandered over to let her know that he had spoken to Regina Clover at the council about the car park, and that her response had been a firm "maybe", but that she would certainly "take any petition into account".

Half an hour later, after she had raked the fallen leaves into two impressive piles and was resisting the urge to jump in them, Dan appeared with Milady for a cup of coffee and a chat before he started his shift. The evenings were starting to draw in, and the wind, when it came now, was a little chilly, but Milady liked to chase Hazel around on the

149

grass, so they sat outside, drinking hot coffee as the wind wrapped around their legs.

'I've seen your petition up all over the place,' Dan told her. 'Great job, there. Me and the dog both signed up. Let's hope it puts an end to this madness.'

'I think it's only a start,' Madeline said. 'I don't know how far it'll go, but I kind of feel like I have to do something.'

Shortly after, Dan called Milady and they headed off across the park. Madeline glanced at her watch, disappointed to see it was nearly half past five and Darren hadn't yet shown up. A dark thought entered her mind that he was trying to give her a little of her own medicine, but she shrugged it off. He wasn't like that, surely?

They hadn't got far enough to exchange numbers, as though the process would somehow bind them into a fledgling relationship. Now Madeline regretted it, as she went back into the café and began to tidy up, wiping off tables and stacking chairs. Hazel, following her inside, weaved around her legs for a while before getting bored and retreating to her tower basket to watch as Madeline, humming forlornly to herself, cleaned and tidied the café ready for the morning.

She checked Hazel's food and water, then cleaned out her litter tray. Then, as she locked up and went out, she couldn't help feeling a wave of disappointment. Did it count as being stood up? They hadn't made a firm arrangement after all. Perhaps he had just got busy.

Be proactive. Go and see him.

So she did, walking up through town towards Darren's veterinary clinic, but when she arrived she found it closed, the car park empty.

Worried that she'd somehow missed him, she hurried back to the park, but there was no one waiting outside. She went inside for a bit and sat with a delighted Hazel, drinking coffee in the easy chair with the lights on, but by seven-thirty no one had shown up, so she finally called it a night and headed for home.

'Not been on the sauce again?' Jonas asked her over breakfast, a wry smile on his face. 'You look darker than those clouds outside.'

Madeline shrugged. 'I'm fine.'

'It's not this car park business, is it? I saw your petition yesterday when I took the car in for an oil change. The car shop had photocopied it from the pharmacy next door. It looks like it's going paper viral, if that's even a thing.'

Madeline forced a smile. 'That's great.'

'It really is. Hopefully the council will take note and put paid to this paid car park nonsense.'

She headed to work under the same thundercloud, but at least felt a little better than before. She barely muttered hello to Pete as he set up his burger van, and Dan as he made one last patrol of the park.

When she got to the café, however, she found a plastic bag hooked up the door handle.

It felt heavy, full of some kind of linen. She weighed it up in one hand while she opened the door and let Hazel out with the other, the cat doing a quick circuit of her legs before racing off across the grass in the pursuit of a falling leaf.

Unable to resist the mystery, she put down a couple of the chairs on the outdoor tables and sat down, opening the bag. Inside was a little unmarked box and a bag of white clothing, marked with the brand of a sports manufacturer.

At the bottom of the bag was a card, the envelope unsealed.

Madeline pulled out the card and turned it over.

A simple design of a cartoon animal walking on crutches told her immediately who it was from.

On the inside was written a short note: *So sorry not to make it over yesterday. Had something personal come up. I'll tell you later. In the meantime, try these on. The final got moved to next Sunday. Last chance before the trophy gets shared. We need you! Dx*

Madeline's mind managed to process the message well enough, but she stared long and hard at the last two figures. It was handwritten, and was that little swirl at the end really an X? There wasn't much else it could be, but she still didn't want to believe it. And if it was supposed to be an X, how should she feel about that? Their relationship had barely gone beyond coffee, vaccinations, and standing each other up.

But if it was an X, it showed clear intent. And the fact that he had given her a present, even one as random as what looked like a set of cricket whites, was another statement. Someone in Australia had once told her you should never give a present to anyone unless you wanted to get involved with that person. Madeline, never a big one for presents, had followed it to the letter ever since.

Now, though, she found herself wanting to give him something back.

She collected Hazel from the lower branches of a tree and carried her back inside, then opened the bag again and had another look at the contents. A brand new set of cricket whites—a size too small for her, but it was a good effort, and Darren had likely gone on the side of caution— and in the box was a brand new shiny cricket ball. The one they had used in the last game had been an old one, battered and scuffed, but this thing of cork, leather, and shiny lacquer was a sporting work of art. She didn't really want to get it dirty.

Such a gift couldn't go unanswered. She cut up a couple of slices of pie, put them into a box, and added half a treacle tart for good measure. Not wanting to be so direct as to address the gift to Darren alone, she added a note that it was for him to share with his staff, then wrapped the box up in a clean tea towel with an oak tree design—one that he would hopefully feel compelled to return—and headed out, luckily catching a bus to speed her the couple of stops up to the clinic. The bus driver, perhaps remembering her from the time she had dived into the road to rescue Hazel, gave her a terse good morning, but when she asked if he had signed the petition to stop the privatisation of the car park, he brightened up and held up a sheet of paper scrawled with a couple of dozen signatures.

She walked back to the park after hanging the tea towel and its contents over the clinic's door, arriving back at the café just in time for opening. Feeling a little better about herself, she took some leftover pie and delivered a slice each to Pete and Dan. Then, humming quietly, she got to work opening the café.

It was a fine morning, the sun breaking through the clouds around ten o'clock, and a cool autumn breeze sending showers of orange leaves cascading across the park. The café was busier than usual with several people dropping in just to try Madeline's newly invented sweet potato and maple tart, which she was pleased to see went down well. Several customers asked if they could order whole tarts to take home. Not wanting to miss the opportunity, Madeline agreed, then made a note to train Ruby on tart making when they had a quiet afternoon.

Ruby arrived at one o'clock, face like a thundercloud,

her mood not helped when a bus of theatre visitors appeared shortly after.

'I had to dump him,' Ruby said, as she stood making coffees beside Madeline.

'Who?'

'Jackson.'

'Who's Jackson?'

'I met him last week. He bought me a Rubik's Cube for our one week's anniversary. He thought it was funny.'

Madeline smiled. 'That's … too bad.'

'It was a lucky escape.'

'You're not going to give him another chance?'

Ruby looked at her and forced a smile. 'No. But don't worry. He has a younger brother.'

'You're going to go out with his younger brother?'

Ruby rolled her eyes. '*No.* To give the Rubik's Cube to. After I threw it at his head.'

'And I thought my life was complicated.'

Ruby shook her head. 'It isn't. It really isn't. Youth these days is a total minefield.'

'I'm starting to see that.'

The side benefit of having a crowd of customers was that they added another twenty or so names to the petition. A couple of customers recalled bad experiences with Snide and Company's car parks, and even added personal notes of dissatisfaction. By the time the group headed over to the theatre for their matinee, Madeline and Ruby were both exhausted but satisfied with how the rush period had gone. The petition notebook had turned another page, and Ruby had picked up a phone number, courtesy of a tidy young man accompanying his elderly grandmother.

'So,' Ruby said, leaning on the doorframe as they watched the last of the customers wandering over to the theatre. 'What's that set of cricket whites in the kitchen about?'

Madeline found herself blushing. 'A present from Darren.'

'Seriously?'

'Yes, seriously. He was planning to stop by last night, but never made it. Then this morning I found those in a bag on the door.'

'Huh. I take it you didn't know his grandmother died yesterday?'

Madeline, walking back through the tables to pick up a stray used cup, almost tripped. 'What?'

'One of his mates posted it on the cricket team social group page. She was in Brentwell Hospital after suffering a stroke several weeks ago. Yesterday afternoon she passed away.'

Madeline had to sit down. She had never got around to asking Darren why he had been in the hospital that day she had thrown the cake at him, but his cheerful demeanour had convinced her it hadn't been for anything serious. Now, the weight of guilt felt like Big Gerry had fallen on her head.

'That's … awful,' she said.

'You know she brought him up, don't you? He never knew his dad and his mum was kind of a waster who died young. His grandmother was everything to him.'

Madeline gave a deflated sigh. *And I thought I had baggage.* 'No,' she said. 'I never knew that.'

'Don't let it get you down. He doesn't talk about it much because he's a forward-thinking kind of guy. I just thought I'd let you know.'

'It sounds like you know him pretty well.'

Ruby shrugged. 'You've got to talk about something when you're batting. You know when the batters meet in the middle between overs? There's only so long you can talk about the weather.'

'I suppose.'

'He probably won't appreciate me telling you, so it might be better to wait until he offers the information, but he seems to like you, so I thought you might as well know.'

Madeline nodded. 'Thanks.'

'Oh, Jesus.'

'What?'

Ruby pointed out through the door. 'Just when you thought the storm was over, here comes another round.'

Madeline stood up. Walking up the path from Big Gerry's mural plaza was a large group of tourists, foreign at a guess from the guide at the front holding up a flag. As she watched, the guide lifted a hand to point at the café. A couple of the tourists checked their watches, then like a giant caterpillar spotting a fresh leaf, as one they began to increase their pace.

'Action stations,' Madeline said. 'I'll drop you a few extra slices of pie for this.'

Ruby grinned. 'You're the best boss ever. I'd better get a gift token in my Christmas card.'

The tourist group stayed most of the afternoon. By the time they were done, Madeline was almost out of stock but the day's takings were not far off what she might have expected for the week. At five o'clock she waved an exhausted Ruby goodbye and flipped the sign to CLOSED. Usually she would stay open another half an hour or so, but her legs were killing her. She scooped up

Hazel and sat down on the easy chair to take a long overdue rest.

She was only halfway through her own well-deserved cup of coffee when someone tapped on the door. She thought about ignoring it, but it might be something important, so she moved Hazel off her lap and got up to check.

Her heart skipped a beat. Darren was peering through the glass panes of the door. When he saw her, he smiled and lifted a hand to wave.

'Hi!' she said, letting him in, unable to keep the smile off her face. Hazel immediately jumped up from the chair and began to circumnavigate his legs. 'Thank you for the, uh, present. I haven't tried them on yet, but I will before Sunday. I'm sure they'll … fit.'

'That's great. And thanks to you for the pie. The staff loved it. So sorry about yesterday, I did mean to come, but something came up.'

'It's okay.' She looked down. 'Ah … Ruby told me about your grandmother.'

Darren's smile dropped. 'Oh.'

'I'm really sorry. And I feel terrible that I didn't know that was why you were in the hospital that day. I'm so sorry I didn't think to ask.'

Darren reached out and took her arm, giving it a gentle squeeze. 'It's quite all right. I mean, we didn't know each other or anything, did we? And you know, it was hard to talk about. I knew it was coming, because she hadn't woken up after the stroke. It was still hard, though. The thing is, I know this sounds stupid, but I've been around a lot of death. It might just be pets, but I know how to balance hope versus reality. I knew she was going, and I was ready.'

'It still must have been hard.'

He was still touching her arm. Madeline figured she might as well return the favour, and before she knew it, she had put one hand over his. He didn't so much as flinch, and it felt so natural that she gave his hand a little squeeze.

'Yeah, it hurt,' Darren said. 'But you know, that's life, isn't it? I mean, not life, but, well, you know.'

'I understand. My mother died just a few weeks before I came home. She had been wheelchair-bound for years. The worst thing was that no one told me. She didn't want to cause any upheaval in my life by dying. It's ridiculous when you think about it.'

'I'm sorry to hear that. Your mother sounds like my grandmother. She would have shooed me away from her bedside if she'd been able. Told me to go out and do something useful.'

'She sounds like a wonderful woman.'

Darren smiled. 'She was, for sure. That wasn't why I didn't show up yesterday, though.'

'No?'

Darren's smile dropped. 'Some scumbag wheel-clamped my car.'

23

NEW FRIENDS AND MORE

'THE HOSPITAL CAR PARK WAS FULL,' Darren said, 'so I had to park in the Pay and Display just up the street. I was in a bit of a hurry, as you might have expected, and when I got back, my car was clamped, for no obvious reason. I called a helpline number on the machine, and after wasting God knows how much money and time getting through a stupid automated system, I finally got in touch with their customer services. All the idiot could tell me was that I had to wait until the clamp guy showed up again.'

'What a nightmare.'

'I waited around for half an hour, then he finally appeared. It turned out I'd been clamped because my car wasn't straight in the space. I wasn't even over the lines, but because my car wasn't straight, according to the company that was breaking some kind of fine print rule. Of course I disputed it, refusing to pay the hundred and fifty quid fine. An absolute joke. We almost got into a fight right there.'

'What did you do? Did you pay it in the end?'

'No chance. I called a mate at Radio Devon, and he called a mate who works for ITV. Half an hour later I had TV cameras down there. No way I was letting those scumbags win. It was on yesterday's news and everything.'

'Sorry, I didn't see it. My dad might have, but I don't watch much television.'

Darren smiled. 'Don't worry. My hair was a mess.'

'Did he let you off?'

'In the end, yeah. Not before I had to create a hell of a fuss on live television. In the end, the guy said he'd release my car as a "goodwill gesture" which took into account my "grief." What an utter, utter scumbag.'

'Let me guess, the car park was owned by Snide and Company?'

'You've got it.' Darren narrowed his eyes. 'Whatever happens, we cannot let the council sell the theatre car park to those devils. Sycamore Park will be ruined.'

'Do you want a coffee?'

'I'd love one. I have something else for you, though.'

'Really?'

'Well, kind of. It's more for Hazel.'

'Hazel?'

Darren smiled. 'Wait a moment.'

He went back outside, and returned with a small carry cage, which he set down on a table. 'I had a visit from Tom this morning,' he said. 'This little chap has a broken wing and needs a bit of nurturing. We're not sure he'll ever be able to fly again, but he should be fine for swimming about. He's only a youngster, though.'

Madeline peered in through the carry cage at a young duck sitting inside. 'You … ah … brought that for Hazel? She's only ever caught butterflies and a few caterpillars.'

Darren laughed. 'No, I don't mean it like that. I was talking to Tom, and he was a little worried that when Hazel gets bigger, she might start targeting the park's birdlife. He thought it might help if she started to see birds as friends.'

'Well, you can try, but I can't guarantee Hazel will go for it.'

Hazel, for her part, was watching with interest from the basket at the top of her cat tower. As both Madeline and the little cat watched, Darren opened the carry cage and took out the little duck. He gave a quack, but otherwise seemed happy enough in Darren's hands.

'His name's Sampson,' Darren said, holding him up towards Hazel. The cat's ears pricked up, her eyes watching the duck intently. Sampson gave a little quack, then, as he came in range, bent to give the cat an exploratory peck. Hazel shifted back, then reached up a paw and gave the duck a pat on the head.

'Let's see how they go on the ground,' Darren said.

He put Sampson down, and the duck began waddling across the floor. Madeline scooped up Hazel, and at first held her close to Sampson, watching her reaction before letting her go. Hazel was perhaps half-grown now, but Sampson was almost as big. As he waddled among chairs, Hazel wandered after him, at first keeping her distance, then slowly getting closer. The duck, quacking contentedly to himself, didn't appear in the least bit alarmed. Finally, as he wandered back in their direction and sat down on the door mat, Hazel wandered over, headbutted him, then slumped down alongside, their bodies pressed together.

'Best friends forever,' Darren said with a smile.

They both felt it best not to risk leaving Hazel and Sampson alone and unsupervised, so Darren returned him to his carry cage, promising to bring him again the following afternoon. Hazel whined at the door as Darren left, wanting her playmate to stay. Madeline, too, was a little sad to see the pair leave, but buoyed by the promise of a swift return.

The next day, Darren showed up just before six o'clock, and they enjoyed coffee and cake together while Hazel and Sampson chased each other among the table legs. It was still too early to leave them alone, but by the time Darren decided it was time to leave, Hazel and Sampson were tucked up together in Hazel's basket by the door, the sleeping cat wrapped like a blanket around the duck. It felt almost cruel to separate them, and when Darren lifted Sampson up to return him to the carry cage, Hazel gave a sad little mew, and Sampson a disappointed quack.

On the Friday afternoon, they decided to take a chance and leave them alone together overnight. Madeline was more nervous than Darren, who had more experience of animal nature, and suggested he treat Madeline to dinner to take her mind off it.

Madeline was sitting opposite him in a nice Italian restaurant near Brentwell Station before it had even crossed her mind that this was a date. Suddenly, the ease with which she had been speaking to Darren before deserted her. Darren returned from the bathroom to find Madeline squirming in her seat, searching for something to say.

'Are you alright?' he asked.

'Ah, yes. It was nice, ah, weather today, wasn't it? Ah … unseasonal?'

Darren smiled. 'A mix of sunny and rainy … so … yes?'

'That's what I thought,' Madeline said. 'That's what I thought, too.'

Darren sat down and reached across the table, putting a hand over hers to stop her fidgeting with a fork.

'Relax,' he said.

'Don't I look relaxed?'

'You look like you've just escaped from prison, and you're just about to get caught.'

'Sorry.'

'Are you worried that this looks like a date?'

Madeline gave a sharp nod. 'Yes.'

Darren smiled again. 'Then you need to overcome your nerves. 'Tell me a secret.'

Madeline frowned. 'Why?'

'Because it'll help you to relax.'

'Ah, give me a minute … all right. I was au-pairing in Australia last year. The parents were away on business as per usual, and one of the kids got a little boisterous one day and knocked over this antique lamp. It split in half. I totally bricked it, and the kids did, too … so I couldn't just dob them in. We went around town, looking for someone to repair it. We managed to find someone in the end, but only when I took the thing in did we find out that there was a small chunk missing, that had broken off the base. I went back and tried to find it, but wherever it had gone, it was lost for all time. In the end I gave up. The restorer guy managed to fix it, even filling in the hole, but if you look closely at the back, you can see where a chunk has been replaced. Once, perhaps when they come to sell it, they'll figure it out.'

Darren chuckled. 'Ouch. Was it expensive?'

'The restorer guy reckoned about twenty grand. The break had made it almost worthless.'

'It sounds like they probably didn't need the money.'

'No, but twenty grand is twenty grand, isn't it?'

'For sure.' He smiled again. 'Nerves gone?'

'Huh. Yes. You're a magician.'

'I wouldn't go that far.'

'Your turn, then.'

'What?'

'Tell me a secret.'

'I don't have any.'

'Yes, you do. Everyone has secrets.'

Darren looked uncomfortable. 'No, I'm a vet. I really don't.'

'Don't lie to me. I can see it in your eyes.'

Darren squeezed his hands together and twisted his head from one side to the other. 'All right. But this is a big one.'

'Go on.'

'I became a vet to made my grandmother happy.'

'Really?'

He looked down. 'My childhood wasn't as conventional as most. My mum was a free spirit, I suppose, if you're being polite about it. I never met my dad and I don't think my mum really knew him either, just one of those fly in, fly out, kind of things. She never even told me his name, but by the time I was five, she was gone, lost to some whim or another. She moved down to London, leaving me with my grandmother, who had never really planned on raising a second child. I think she blamed herself for my mother's inability to do the motherly thing, and did her best to stumble through. I had no brothers or sisters though, so it was hard for her to entertain me. I told you about Jim, didn't I?'

'Your dog? He was a beagle, wasn't he?'

Darren gave a fond smile. 'That's right. My grandmother basically bought him for me because I had no brothers or sisters. I loved that dog so much. He was the best pet ever, and I was heartbroken when he died. My grandmother lamented the local vet's inability to first diagnose the cancer, and second, to treat it. I told you I promised myself that I would become a vet, so that I could stop other children going through the same heartache, but it was my grandmother who suggested it. I think I was angry about Jim's death, and that was her way of helping me to deal with it. The idea got stuck in my head, and stayed there.'

'But your heart was never in it?'

'I convinced myself that it was. I chose a path in life, and I lowered my head and stuck to that path, but it wasn't until I'd literally qualified as a vet, that I began to doubt myself. My grandmother, however, was so proud. There was no way I could ever let her down.'

'You felt bound by duty?'

'I did. I set up my own clinic, and grew it, to the point that I have two junior vets working beneath me, both extremely competent. When I look at it from the outside, though, I sometimes wonder if I've built the business that way so that it can continue to exist after I break away to do my own thing. I'm still not sure that I've found my path, you know?'

Madeline gave a furtive nod. 'I've been jumping back and forth from different paths for my whole adult life. For a while I think I'm heading in the right direction, then I either get cold feet or I get scared of commitment and take a jump off somewhere else.'

'But I think that's okay,' Darren said. 'I don't think you have to follow the same way forever. I don't think that's what life's about. It's what we've convinced ourselves that it's about, but that's just society's way of keeping order. I think things are a little more complicated than that.'

Madeline had put her hands over Darren's without

even realising it. Now, with a coy look towards a waiter standing nearby, she said, 'Do you think we'd better order?'

Madeline was a little concerned about Hazel and Sampson, so Darren offered to walk her home, cutting through Sycamore Park on the way so that she could check on the two animals. Using a phone light to peer through the window, they saw the two cuddled up together in the basket at the top of the cat tower.

'I wonder how Sampson got up there?' Darren asked. 'I suppose he must have hopped.'

'Where there's a will, there's a way,' Madeline said.

On the far side of the park, they bumped into Dan, patrolling with Milady. Darren gave a gasp of fright at the sight of the one-eyed nightwatchman approaching out of the foggy gloom beneath the nearest street light, but Madeline, a little tipsy from too much wine, just laughed. Recognising Madeline, Dan dropped his fearsome scowl and wished them goodnight.

They walked on out of the park and across to Redfield. At the end of Madeline's road, she paused.

'I'll be okay from here,' she said. 'My house is just up there. Thanks so much for tonight.'

'It was my pleasure. I hope we can do it again soon. I hope we can do it again lots of times. I … really like you, Madeline.'

Her heart felt like it was going to explode. Madeline trembled as Darren lifted a finger to stroke the side of her face. He began to lean closer … just as a thunderous rumble came from overhead, and fat drops of rain began to fall.

Darren gave a reluctant grimace and pulled away. 'I'd better let you go,' he said, as the rain began to intensify.'

'Do you want an umbrella? I might have one you can borrow.'

'It's fine. I don't want to wake your dad. I'll see you soon, okay?'

'For sure.'

Darren reached out and squeezed her hand. Madeline didn't want to let go, but the rain was starting to intensify. She pulled away, waving as Darren hurried back up the street, pulling his jacket up over his head. As he reached the corner, he turned back and waved, then he was gone, running out of sight. Madeline watched him a moment longer, then turned and ran for home.

24

CONFESSIONS

AFTER THE RAIN the night before, Sycamore Park was fresh and lush the next morning, basking under a clear blue October sky. Pete had taken the weekend off to do catering for a wedding, but Dan stopped by for a piece of cake and a coffee before going home, then Tom stopped in to ask how Hazel was getting on with her new friend. Madeline pointed to the pair chasing each other around the base of a tree trunk.

'I think your ducks are probably safe from my tiger,' she said.

Ruby arrived just after lunchtime, but with the park unseasonably warm after the overnight storm, most customers were after takeaways to eat and drink out on the grass under the falling leaves, so the café itself was quiet. At just after five, Madeline decided to close up for the evening. With an hour or so of decent light left, Ruby offered to give her some catching practice with the cricket ball Darren had given her.

Once she had got over the initial hardness of the ball thudding into her palms, Madeline began to rediscover a little of her teenage sportiness, even if throwing a ball so heavy and hard made her arm felt like it was popping out of its socket.

Ruby had to go off to meet some student friends, and Darren had told Madeline Saturdays were usually his busiest day at work, so Madeline went back to the café, made herself a coffee, and sat outside at one of the tables, watching Hazel and Sampson play among the leaves. The evening was drawing in, the air starting to chill, but sitting there, watching the cat and duck playing together, Madeline felt more peaceful and content than she had since getting off the plane nearly two months ago. The pieces of her life, it seemed, were finally starting to line up.

She was just thinking of going home, when a figure appeared, walking quickly up the path in the café's direction. As soon as she recognised the man, Madeline thought to duck out of sight, but it was too late, he had already seen her. She could do nothing but sit and wait as Rory marched up to her table and plonked his briefcase down in front of her.

'God, what a day,' he said.

'Oh, hi, Rory,' she muttered, having barely thought about him all week. She remembered with a little bit of guilt that she had provisionally agreed to host his wedding, all the while trying to break his company behind his back.

'You won't believe the hell I've been going through,' he said. 'Honestly, I feel like someone's got a vendetta on my head.'

'That bad?' Madeline said, sitting up and trying to look innocent.

'We're friends, aren't we?' Rory said. 'I mean, we go way back. I can trust you, can't I?'

'Uh ... yeah.'

'It's Janine. I think she wants to pull the wedding.'

'Really?'

Rory leaned forwards. 'Between you and me, I think she's got a little flustered by all this petition rubbish, and is getting cold feet.'

'Ah … what petition rubbish?'

Rory flapped a hand. 'Don't worry about it. Some scumbag is taking a pot shot at my company, trying to save that useless patch of tarmac over there by the theatre. Probably some clown who can't park straight. Don't they know what's good for them? More spaces equal more customers. And Snide and Company will maintain the car park far better than those idiots at the council. No more weeds, no more wildflowers. And proper surveillance. No one trying to camp out, causing trouble.'

'Sounds … lovely.' Madeline stood up. 'Can you … hang on a minute?' She shrugged. 'Nature, and all that.'

'Oh, sure.'

Remembering something Ruby had said, she hurried back into the cafe. Then, as soon as she was out of sight, she pulled out her phone and set up the voice recorder. Slipping it back into her pocket, she went back outside to the table.

'Sorry about that.'

'No problem.'

'So … you were saying? I mean, you want to buy the car park, don't you? Are you sure that's a good idea? A lot of people aren't happy, by the look of things.'

'They just don't know what's good for them. People need rules. For example, that's the theatre car park, right? How many people likely park there and walk into town, because it's free?'

'I imagine quite a few. It's not that far, and there's no free parking in the town centre.'

'Exactly. They're cheapskates.'

'What is wrong with free parking?'

Rory rolled his eyes. 'It's a wasted business opportunity.'

'I don't ever remember you being so … cutthroat.'

'I did what I needed to do. We all do. Did you prefer it when I lived in a caravan in my parents' front garden? I now have a nice three-bedroom apartment in the centre of town. I drive a nice car. What do you drive?'

'Uh….' Madeline smiled. '… I drive customers into the café.'

'So, all those years of travelling and finding yourself—' Here Rory made quotation marks with his fingers while rolling his eyes at the same time, '—and you've achieved what, exactly? Do you have a pension plan? Stocks? Savings?'

'That'll be … none of the above.'

'Well, congratulations on being a free spirit. People might hate me, but they envy me at the same time.'

Madeline decided to change tack. 'So … no disrespect, but your company doesn't have a great reputation. I've heard of a couple of people getting tickets for really minor things.'

'It'll teach them to park better next time.'

'And that you have no customer services for people to call?'

Rory laughed. 'Of course we do, but you have to get through the automated system first, and believe me, not many people can figure that out. Not my problem, though. That's nothing to do with me. My job is purchasing new real estate, not wasting my time with a few whiny motorists. They need to just shut up and pay up.'

'I overheard one customer saying they'd been fined nearly two hundred pounds after the machine refused to print their ticket.'

'They're a liar. The world is full of them. Please don't be so gullible.'

'So … you don't have any respect for your customers?'

'Why should I? They're just bags of money waiting to be opened.' He grinned. 'And if they happen to stray over the lines, we'll squeeze out a little extra.'

Rory's eyes had taken on a crazed tint that had Madeline flinching back. Surely, the man she had once been in a relationship with was long gone, his soul consumed by power and greed.

'Don't you think that's a little … immoral?'

Rory shrugged. 'It's just business.'

'Right.'

'But, anyway, we were talking about Janine.'

'Oh, of course.'

Rory sighed. 'I think she wants to call off the wedding.'

'She's said that?'

'Not in so many words. You know how these therapists are. It's all smoke and mirrors. She'll say something like, "I'm not sure if being a November bride is good for business", which basically means she wants to call it off.'

'That's too bad.'

'If only I could get this petition rubbish to go away.'

'Well, I know one way,' Madeline began, wondering if fluttering her eyelids might make her more endearing. 'You could cancel the plan to—'

'Mind if I use your bathroom?' Rory said, standing up.

'No problem.'

'Thanks.'

He went inside. Certain that she had enough of a "confession" to satisfy Ruby, Madeline pulled out her phone and switched off the voice recorder. She was just putting it back into her pocket when she got the sense of someone standing behind her.

'What the hell do you call this?'

Before Madeline could turn, a sheaf of papers and notebooks slapped down on the tabletop in front of her. She closed her eyes, wishing she'd thought to put them out of sight, but she hadn't expected Rory to go into the café. Caught up in her efforts to catch him, he had caught her.

'I get that you might have put out that book just so people didn't get the hump,' Rory said. 'You know, doing your hippy bit, and all that. But what's this?' He flipped open one of the notebooks to the back, to where Madeline had written a list of participating businesses.

'Ah, just a little reminder—'

'It was you, wasn't it?' Rory said. 'You're the mastermind behind this stupid petition.' He did the finger quotes again, this time around mastermind. 'I thought we were close, Madeline.'

'We're not close, Rory. You're my ex-boyfriend. We broke up eight years ago. And for what it's worth, I think you should leave the theatre car park alone.'

Rory shook his head. He flapped his hands up and down, his face puckering. One foot stamped up and down.

Madeline almost smiled. Some people didn't really change after all.

'It's not fair!' Rory shouted, stamping his foot again. With one hand he swiped the petition off the table in front of her and began to rip it to pieces, lines of signatures and addresses fluttering in the breeze. As he ranted, Madeline wished she'd left the voice recorder running. 'It's not fair at all! I—'

Oh my god, he's really going to say it.

'—*hate* you!'

'Rory, I think you should go home.'

'Don't worry. I'm going. And I'm *not* having my wedding at your stupid café. In fact, I might just have my company buy your café, then raze it to the ground. A few more parking spaces will be much more useful than your horrible drinks.'

Madeline just waited as he picked up his briefcase and stomped away across the park. He looked back once, flapping a hand at her in some weird, childlike expression of disappointment. As soon as he was out of sight, Madeline retrieved the shredded petition as best she could, then collected Hazel and Sampson from where they were playing—completely unconcerned by the meltdown that had happened nearby—among the fallen leaves.

'It's all right for you two,' Madeline said, as she took the two animals back into the café and set them down on the floor. 'It's pretty unlikely that I've heard the end of this.'

25

IT'S JUST CRICKET

IT WAS a fine morning for a cricket match, the sun shining over the top of the small pavilion, as the players milled around outside, excited to get on with the tournament final at long last. Madeline, trying to feel enthusiastic in her shiny new cricket whites—which had proven, to her surprise, to be a perfect fit—stood by the boundary line and watched two players dragging a rope across the playing field to remove the morning dew.

'Hey, I was wondering where you were.'

She looked up to see Darren, also dressed in his whites, striding towards her. As he reached her, he gave her arm a gentle squeeze.

'Hi.'

'You don't look so great. Is everything all right?'

Madeline forced a smile, then let it drop. 'No.'

'Let's go over there, behind the scorebox.'

Madeline let him lead her along the pitch until they were out of the earshot of the other players.

'Tell me what's wrong.'

Madeline did. By the time she had finished, she was sobbing against his shoulder as he patted her back.

'He's a clown. Just forget about him.'

'It's … it's nothing like that. It's just the nerve of the man.'

'Don't worry. He won't get that car park, and he won't get the café either. If it helps, I'll call up the local medical professionals association. They might have some clout with the council. And if that doesn't work, we can contact the local MP. Somehow or other, we'll kick Snide and Company right out of town.'

'Thanks. I appreciate it.'

'Come on, I think it's time for the team pep talk.'

Madeline wiped her eyes, trying to look normal as they went back to the pavilion, where the rest of the team had gathered. Ruby, her hair freshly snow-white with silver streaks running through it, gave Madeline a thumbs up.

'Right, statistically, we're screwed,' Ruby's dad said. 'They've won more games than us this season, we haven't beaten them in three years, and we only have nine players. Potentially ten, but I'm not yet sure if the umpires will allow Donald's dog to take the field. But, going by the simple odds, we might as well just hand over the trophy right now.' He grinned. 'But that's not going to happen, is it?'

'No!' the team shouted in unison, Madeline just a little out of time, but raising a fist for emphasis.

'Good. You know me. I work with numbers, so as far as I'm concerned, we're going to lose. But the rest of you, you work with heart. And what are we going to do?'

'Smash them!' everyone shouted, except for Madeline, who chimed in with a sturdy, 'Win!'

Ruby's dad had lost the coin toss, and the other team chose to bat first. Madeline was sent out to the boundary edge to field, and was pleased to stay out of much of the action. The only time a ball came sailing towards her, accompanied by frantic shouts of 'Catch it! Catch it!' it ended up flying far over her head and landing in the field beyond. Feeling obliged, she began to pick her way through stinging nettles in a vain attempt to retrieve it, but Darren came running over with a smile on his face and told her that one was for the cows.

Once a replacement ball had been discovered, the game continued, and by the end of the innings, the opposition had amassed a challenging total.

'Right,' Ruby's dad said in the team huddle before the players went out to bat. 'We've somehow got to chase down a hundred and ninety. Who remembers the best score we've chased this year?'

'A hundred and fifty-five,' one man said.

'And who remembers the last time we chased a total as big as this?'

'1985?' someone quipped, to nervous laughter.

Ruby's dad didn't laugh. '2004,' he said. 'So statistically, the odds are not in our favour. How are we going to overcome that?'

There were shrugs, a few mutters of 'Try harder?' and a couple of nervous laughs.

Madeline, feeling buoyed by not having dropped any catches or having made any obvious mistakes, stuck up a hand.

'Er, Mary, yes?'

'Madeline.'

'Madeline, sorry. How do you think we're going to win this?'

'If we win, there's a free coffee for everyone at the Oak Leaf Café in Sycamore Park this afternoon.'

There were a few murmurs of approval.

'Plus a fresh slice of treacle tart!' Ruby shouted.

'I haven't made any!' Madeline whispered to her as a series of cheers went up.

'We'll buy some from the supermarket,' Ruby whispered back, as someone else shouted, 'With cream?'

'Cream, whipped cream, clotted cream, or ice cream!' Ruby shouted.

'All of it?' asked Ivy the huge spin bowler, a hopeful look on her face.

'Only if we win!' Ruby shouted.

'Win! Win! Win!' came a chorus of shouting, as the players patted their knees in unison.

'Right, let's go,' Ruby's dad said. 'Rubik, Darren, get out there.'

Against some good bowling, Milton Road's team made a fairly sedate start. Darren didn't last long, taking a horrid swipe in an attempt to relieve some pressure and getting caught out on the boundary. He shook his head and grimaced as he came in, tossing his bat on the ground.

'Should have been six,' he said. 'We're never going to win this.'

'Don't give up,' Madeline said, just as the next wicket fell, the batter out first ball to a huge cheer from the other team. 'Well, not just yet.'

'While Ruby's there, we've got a chance,' Darren said. 'She's strangely sedate, though. She needs to be fired up.'

He had barely finished speaking when the next batter was out, caught second ball, the fielding team going crazy with excitement. As the next Milton Road player scrambled to get their pads on and out onto the pitch, Darren sighed.

'At least you won't have to give out a load of free coffees.'

Madeline patted him on the arm. 'Have a little faith. I haven't batted yet.'

'Have you ever batted before?'

'Nope. How hard can it be?'

'Just hit it,' Darren said, patting her on the shoulder. 'That's all you've got to do, really.'

For a while, Milton Road looked like they might have a chance. Ruby and her dad steadied things for a while, creeping them closer. When Ruby's dad was out, there were still thirty runs to get and only Ivy and Madeline left to bat. The team cheered for Ivy as she lumbered out, sweat already streaming down her face.

'Come on, Ivy!' Madeline called. 'Good luck!'

'Just hit it!' Darren shouted.

'Is she any good?' Madeline asked as she shifted awkwardly in the leg pads Darren had helped her strap on.

Darren gave her a pained look. 'She's scored three runs all season,' he said, and that was off an inside edge. 'Right, here we go.'

The bowler ran in.

Ivy's bat scythed through the air, striking the ball with a hearty clump. It sailed through the air, flying high over the pavilion and landing in the hedge.

Cheers went up from Milton Road's players. Ivy, who had walked up the pitch a few steps, seemed to give Madeline a long stare before going back to her mark.

'She's doing it for the treacle tart,' Darren said. 'What a legend. She's probably got one eye on the most improved player trophy as well.'

The bowler came in again, and Ivy's bat swung, this time hacking across the line of the ball to send it sailing away behind the wickets, this time landing in a ditch. Milton Road's players danced with joy while the opposition retrieved it from the mud and wiped it on the grass.

On the next ball, however, Ivy's luck ran out, as she sent the ball steepling high into the air. As the ball hovered, Milton Road's players got their hopes up, but the opposition captain took a good catch, and Ivy was out.

'You're in,' Darren said to Madeline. 'See if you can get Ruby fired up. And when you're facing, just try to hit it.'

'Just hit it,' Madeline said, trying to give him a thumbs up in the thick, padded cricket glove. 'I'll try.'

The other team clapped her as she walked out to the middle of the field. It was the first time she had batted in a cricket game since perhaps a casual affair at primary school, and she only remembered what she had to do from watching the other players.

As she reached the wicket, Ruby came wandering over to offer some advice.

'We've got eight balls left and we need eighteen to win. 'It's tough, but it's not impossible. Two balls left this over, and you're on strike. Just don't get out and I'll deal with it the next over.'

Madeline smiled. 'Stay in and don't get out?'

'Yeah, that's about it.'

Madeline remembered something Darren had said about firing Ruby up. 'My ex-boyfriend showed up yesterday, after you'd gone,' she said. 'He found out about the petition and had a bit of a wobbly.'

'No!'

'Yeah.'

'Are you alright?'

'I'm fine. But he wasn't very nice about it.' She smiled. 'Can you do me a favour as it's probably a little beyond my ability? Imagine his face on the ball for a bit.'

Ruby's gaze darkened. 'My pleasure.'

With Ruby chomping at the bit, Madeline had to go back and face the next ball. The bowling didn't look that fast from the safety of the pavilion, but the first ball zipped past so fast she barely even saw it before it thumped into the wicketkeeper's gloves and the opposition gave a cheer.

'Rubbish, this one,' said a fielder standing nearby. 'Our name's already on the trophy, lads.'

Madeline stared at him. The voice sounded familiar from somewhere … her cheeks flushed. It was him, Adam Wright, the man who she had knocked off the bike. Perhaps he hadn't recognised her before—

The next ball zipped past her before she'd even realised it was being bowled. The opposition let out a series of 'oohs', then the fielders began to change over ready for the last over to begin. Just before he moved to his new fielding position, Adam Wright fixed her with a stare.

'You,' he said. 'Cake shop girl.'

For a moment the air seemed to go still, and Madeline felt like a gunslinger facing off against a dueling opponent. The twang of Wild Western music seemed to fill the air.

'Best cakes in Brentwell,' she said, holding his stare. Then, caught up in the heat of battle, she narrowed her eyes. 'Winners' cakes,' she added. '*Cup* winners' cakes.'

'Adam, get a move on!' the opposition captain said, and the spell was broken, Adam giving her one last glare before moving to his new fielding position.

'What are you doing?' Ruby asked, coming down to talk to her.

Madeline gave her a defiant smile. 'Oh, just getting into things,' she said.

'We need eighteen to win,' Ruby said. 'Don't worry, I'll deal with this.'

'Good,' Madeline said. 'I'm happy to watch from the non-striker's end.'

Everyone got into position for the last over. Madeline, standing at the non-striker's end beside the umpire, waited as the bowler ran in. Ruby, on strike, scowled as the ball came down, then stepped out and took a massive swing. The ball cracked against the bat and went sailing over the infield, out towards the boundary. A fielder ran after it, but it was no good. It flew over the rope for six runs. Milton Road's players cheered.

Just twelve to win.

Ruby smashed the next ball back past the bowler, and screamed at Madeline to run. The outfield was still damp, so the grass slowed the ball down enough to be fielded before it reached the boundary, but they managed to run two.

Ten to win, with four balls remaining.

The next ball was a filthy long hop, bouncing up around Ruby's shoulder. Like a seasoned pro, Ruby swivelled, catching the ball on the rise, and sent it sailing over the boundary towards the pavilion. It narrowly missed the pavilion's windows, bouncing off the wall for six more runs.

Three balls left, four to win, and suddenly, for perhaps the first time in the game, it looked like Milton Road were favourites. Between balls, Ruby came down the wicket to give Madeline some advice.

'Whatever happens, just run,' she said.

'Got it.'

The next ball was a little wide, and Ruby should have

left it, getting the extra run for a wide ball, but caught up in the heat of battle, she reached out and took a swipe at it, catching it with the toe of the bat. The ball ran away behind the wickets. Madeline screamed, 'Run!' and came charging down the pitch. Ruby, caught unawares, was slow to start. The fielder, seeing she was a long way short of her ground, attempted to throw the ball to the bowler's end, but missed, and the ball ran away into the outfield.

'Run!' Ruby screamed, making a quick turn as the fielders ran off in pursuit of the misbehaving throw.

Madeline ran the second run hard, then turned and started for a third before even looking up at Ruby. As she made her ground to complete the run, she realised what she had done, putting herself on strike with two balls left and one run needed. As the fielders got back into position, Ruby watched her helplessly from the non-striker's end.

'This one couldn't hit a deadline,' Adam Wright said to the other fielders, as they all moved closer. 'Catching practice here, boys. Can't bat, can't … *cook.*'

'How would you know?' Madeline said.

'Concentrate!' Ruby shouted from the non-striker's end, and Madeline dragged her eyes away from Adam Wright just in time to see the ball come zooming towards her. More out of an attempt to protect herself than anything else, she took a massive swipe at the ball, somehow stuck it with the back of her bat, and stared in dismay as it flew straight towards where Adam Wright stood a few metres away.

It was an easy catch. All he had to do was hold his hands still, but as the ball went into his hands, he leaned back, and his feet slipped on the grass. He fell backwards, and the ball popped out, rolling across the grass.

The Milton Road players cheered. Adam Wright

jumped up, protesting to the umpires about poor playing conditions.

'All right, back to your positions,' the umpire said, as Adam Wright glared at Madeline.

'Lucky there,' he said. 'You won't get lucky twice.'

'Ignore that clown!' Ruby shouted, coming down the wicket as the bowler walked back to his mark to prepare for the last ball of the match. 'Concentrate,' she hissed. 'This is the last ball, and the scores are tied. They lost less wickets, though, so they win if the scores finish like this. You just have to get back on it and I'll run like hell. Just get your head down and get to the other end. Got it?'

Madeline forced a smile, but inside she was a bundle of nerves. 'I'll do my best.'

'It's over to you now,' Ruby said. 'Do you want to go down in club folklore, or do you want to spend the rest of your life polishing a second place medal?'

'We get medals?'

'I don't know. I suppose it depends on the league association's budget.'

'Can we please get on with the game?' shouted the umpire.

Ruby patted Madeline on the shoulder. 'Good luck.'

'Thanks.'

As Ruby ran back to her end of the pitch, Madeline tapped her bat on the ground and stared at the bowler about to run in. She was acutely aware of Adam Wright chirping at her from a few feet away. Something about how if she couldn't see a bicycle, she had no chance at seeing a ball. She thought of Rory, stomping his feet and ripping up her petition.

There really were a lot of idiots in the world. In some ways she felt sorry for the poor ball—

'Hit it!'

It bounced midway down the pitch and came steepling for her face. Madeline threw up her bat, shut her eyes. She missed the ball completely, instead feeling it bounce off her shoulder with a sharp stab of pain.

'Ow!'

'*Run!*'

Madeline opened her eyes to see Ruby racing towards her. She started forwards, dropped and tripped over her bat, sprawling forwards onto the pitch. Then, with Ruby nearly upon her, she scrambled to her feet.

Behind her, someone was shouting for the fielder to throw the ball to the non-striker's end. Madeline was still miles away from safety, and a fielder had come to stand behind the stumps. Aware she was racing against a ball she couldn't see, Madeline closed her eyes and tried to summon one of her old bursts of speed, the ones she had loved at the end of a tough cross-country race, where you empty out the tank for one last push for the line. The safety crease became the finish line, and Madeline found herself grinning.

One more step—

The ball bounced in beside her, the fielder reaching to gather it. As he collected the ball and pulled it across to break the stumps, Madeline got a foot over the line.

Milton Road's players erupted in a massive cheer. Madeline stumbled to safety, looking up to see the dismay on Adam Wright's face as he broke the wicket just a second too late.

Her momentum had sent her sprawling. As she rolled over and sat up, Adam Wright came over and extended a hand.

'Well played, cake girl,' he said, offering her a grim smile.

Madeline had blood ringing in her ears. She smiled

back and took his hand. 'Oak Leaf Café in Sycamore Park,' she said. 'We also have second-place cakes, and they taste just as good. Everyone welcome.'

Adam smiled. 'Good game,' he said. 'We'll see you all there.'

26

RESCUE

AFTER THE GAME, there was a presentation of the Sunday League Cup to Milton Road, followed by some speeches by the captains. Despite the intensity of the game, as soon as it was over everyone was laughing and joking with each other. Adam Wright even came over to apologise to Madeline for the way he had spoken to her in the hospital. With Darren looking on in the background, Madeline didn't have the heart to tell him that it had probably worked out for the best.

Later, she repeated her offer that everyone was welcome back at the Oak Leaf Café for coffee and cake. A few players wanted to go home and change first, so they arranged a time for three o'clock. It was only just after lunchtime, so Madeline needed to get back and rush-make a couple of treacle tarts. Ruby and Darren offered to accompany her.

With the sun shining, Sycamore Park was in the full grip of a colourful autumn day. Falling leaves drifted through the air, swirling around dog walkers, joggers, couples and families out for a Sunday afternoon stroll.

187

With the café temporarily closed, Pete was doing a roaring trade out of thRory, with a dozen people queued up. As they walked up through the park to the café, Madeline had a wide smile on her face.

Everything was rosy….

'Madeline,' Ruby said. 'What's happened to the window?'

The reflection of the sunlight wasn't quite right, and as Madeline quickened her pace, she saw Ruby was right, there was something wrong with the window just to the left of the entrance. The lattice window, nine panes, was now missing one. Parts of it glittered from the ground below.

'Someone's put a rock through it,' Darren said.

Madeline unlocked the door and went inside. A large stone lay on the floor under one of the tables, and other pieces of glass lay underneath the broken window. Luckily it was a small pane of glass that wouldn't cost too much to fix, but still … that someone had vandalized the café made Madeline seethe with anger.

'How dare they?' she said, clenching her fists together. It didn't look like anyone had tried to get in, but—'Oh my god. Where are they?'

Ruby had gone into the kitchen while Darren waited by the door. 'Here's Sampson,' Ruby said, returning with the little duck nestled in her arms. 'But where's Hazel?'

'She must have got out through the hole,' Madeline said, feeling her knees tremble. 'Oh my god, where is she?'

Dan had already gone home, but Pete was happy to close thRory in order to join the search, along with Lizzie from the library, and a handful of other passersby who wondered who they were searching for. Starting from the café, they moved outwards, calling the little cat's name, looking in bushes and peering up into trees. Madeline's biggest fear was that Hazel might have run onto the road, but a search that way found nothing. She could only hope that Hazel was hiding somewhere nearby.

As the search lengthened, she slowly began to lose hope. At best, someone might have found the little cat wandering around, thought she was a friendly stray, and taken her home. At worst … Madeline didn't want to think about it.

Then, just as they were about to give up, Lizzie, standing beneath the huge leaning trunk of Big Gerry, pointed up into the tree.

'Look. There she is, right up there.'

Hazel had somehow managed to climb up Big Gerry's massive trunk and out on to a bough that overhung the path. She now sat, seemingly unconcerned, three metres above their heads.

'How are we going to get her down?' Ruby asked.

'Give her a poke with a stick or something,' Pete suggested. 'She's a cat. She'll be fine.' As if to disagree, Hazel gave a sad little meow.

'Can you tempt her down with some fish?' Lizzie said.

It was worth a try. They placed a bowl of cat food at the base of Big Gerry's trunk, then hooked a piece of tuna fish out of a sandwich Pete had made himself for lunch on to a paperclip, which they then taped to a bamboo pole from Angela's little garden. Even with it waved in front of her face, however, Hazel wouldn't move.

'If we get a net or something, perhaps we can push her off,' Ruby suggested, but no one had a net. Pete went to see if Tom had a ladder in his shack, but it was Tom's day off and the shack was locked.

'We could walk up to the hardware store on Devon Road and see if we can borrow one,' Darren said.

'My dad might have one in his garden,' Madeline said. She pulled out her phone and called Jonas, but he had gone to a rugby match and could only remember having lent his ladder to someone, but couldn't remember who.

'My brother Gus will have one,' Pete said. 'I'll have to go all the way back to Willow River to get it, though.'

This seemed like the best idea, and Pete was just about to set off, when the unthinkable happened. A sparrow landed on a branch a little further out on the bough, and Hazel, with a cheerful meow, began to climb after it, getting higher and higher, the branches beneath her feet getting thinner and thinner. At one point she slipped and nearly fell, but managed to right herself with a deft twist and scamper a little further out along the branch. As she bounced through thinner branches, yellow and brown leaves fluttered down around the group below.

'I think we have no choice but to call in the cavalry,' Pete said. 'Hopefully the lads at the fire brigade are having a quiet morning.'

At that moment, the two cricket teams arrived, having car pooled to the park after doing a supermarket run for a few beers to drink with their cakes out on the grass. Some had changed out of their gear, some still wore it, their knees and elbows grass stained, their thighs marked with red smears from where they had been rubbing the cricket ball.

'Got a cat stuck up a tree,' Pete said by way of greeting. 'No one's an off-duty fireman, by any chance?'

It turned out that one of the opposition team actually was, and made a call on his mobile to a mate currently on duty. However, Brentwell's fire service was currently dealing with a warehouse fire on the other side of town and would be unable to rescue any stuck cats for the next couple of hours.

'I still think the stick and a net is the best option,' Pete said.

'Statistically more likely to lead to success,' Ruby's dad added.

At that moment, things took another turn for the worse. The sparrow returned, fluttering among the outmost branches of the protruding bough. Hazel, who had again been sitting quite peacefully in a crook between two branches, now let out a little mew of delight and took off, running out towards the end of the branch. The sparrow took off out of range, leaving the cat clambering among the leafless twigs. She tried to turn round, slipped, and her back legs dropped through. She clung on with her front paws but her back ones scrabbled uselessly.

'She's going to fall!' Ruby shouted.

'We can catch her,' Pete said.

'It's too high!' Lizzie shouted. 'What if we miss?'

It was Ivy who stepped up. 'Human pyramid,' she said, clenching a fist. 'I'll be the core.'

Ivy squatted down on one powerful knee. At first no one really knew what to do, then Lizzie, who had apparently once been a member of a dance club, began to organise people around her, everyone holding each other steady. Madeline, Ruby, and Margaret from the cricket club climbed on top of Ivy's broad shoulders, supported by the other players around her.

They were still a couple of metres below Hazel's dangling body, the cat new meowing with distress as she failed to regain her spot on the branch.

'I'm a vet,' Darren said. 'Let me get her.'

Helped by others, he climbed up on to the first layer of the pyramid, then Madeline, Ruby and Margaret cupped their hands together to lift his feet. With the whole structure on the verge of collapse, he rose towards the stricken cat.

'Just a little more … come on, a little higher … just … got her!'

He managed to get a hand on Hazel just as the whole structure gave way. Bodies sprawled everywhere. As he fell, Darren passed Hazel to Madeline, who managed to scramble out of the way. Darren was not so lucky, going down hard in the middle of the crush.

The two cricket teams cheered. Hazel, clearly missing Sampson, wriggled out of Madeline's arms and scampered back towards the café. Everyone was patting Ivy on the back and congratulating her on her plan, when Madeline noticed Darren sitting on the edge of the grass verge, clutching his ankle.

'Are you alright?'

He winced as he looked up at her. 'I think it's broken,' he said.

27

REPAIRS AND REBUILDING

MADELINE LEFT Ruby in charge of the café, with Ivy and Margaret stepping up to help with coffees and cakes, while Pete offered free burgers to anyone a little hungrier. Then, getting a lift from Lizzie, Madeline went with Darren to Brentwell General Hospital.

'Isn't it ironic that this is the place where we first met?' Darren said with a pained smile, as Madeline helped him into a wheelchair provided for patients by the main doors. 'Although I'd prefer to see a little less of this place, to be honest.'

Madeline, trying not to think about the way he had said it, as though they were in a relationship already, concentrated on pushing the chair, hoping none of the passing nurses could see her blushing.

The hospital was quiet for a Sunday, and they didn't have to wait long. Darren was given an X-ray and examined, and found only to have a bad strain. The doctor put the ankle into a cast anyway, then told Darren to get plenty of rest.

'You look after him,' the doctor said to Madeline, making her blush again. 'Make sure he takes plenty of rest at home, but don't let him overeat.'

'I'll … er … try,' Madeline said, much to Darren's amusement.

As they came out of the hospital, they waved at Lizzie, waiting in the short-stay spaces across from the entrance.

'At least Snide and Company hasn't spread its web this far yet,' Darren said. 'Although I imagine it won't be long.'

'The doctor said you should rest,' Madeline said. 'Would you like me to ask Lizzie to take you home?'

Darren shook his head. 'Well, since I'm a vet, and that's kind of a doctor, I'll take my own advice, which is to go back to the party.'

'I have an easy chair you can use.'

He smiled. 'That would be great.'

The party was in full swing. Some of the cricket players sat around in the café, others were out on the grass, drinking beer, eating burgers and cakes. Hazel and Sampson were chasing each other through the trees, closely watched by Ivy. A huge cheer went up as Darren and Madeline arrived. Beers and cakes were offered, but Darren was feeling a little sore and tired, so Madeline helped him into the easy chair inside the café, then went to help Ruby, who was struggling to juggle everyone's orders. As Madeline came outside, carrying a tray of coffees and cakes, Adam Wright came over, a sheepish grin on his face.

'I just wanted to say sorry again for being rude and calling you a stupid hippy,' he said.

Madeline smiled. 'It's all right.'

'No, I was out of order. I wanted to make it up to you, if I can. While on weekends I'm a wild, rule-ignoring cyclist, during the week I'm a professional glazier. I see you have a little problem with one of your windows, and I'd be happy to repair it, for free, of course. I'd always be happy to give the rest of them a check over, make sure you're all good with sealant and everything before the winter comes.'

Madeline beamed. 'That's so nice of you. Thank you.'

'And your cakes are awesome, by the way. The best in Brentwell.'

'Thank you so much.' She held out the tray. 'Why don't you have another piece?'

'I'd be delighted. Thanks.'

Slowly, the party began to wind down. The players drifted off in ones and twos, some to go home, a few hardcore heading off to town centre pubs to continue their afterparty. Pete went off to close down the burger van, Lizzie headed back to the library. Madeline waved goodbye to Ruby and her dad, both laden down with wrapped slices of pie and tart, and finally it was only herself and Darren left.

Adam had promised to come first thing Monday morning to replace the window pane, but before leaving he had cleared up the broken glass and fitted a piece of plywood into the gap. Madeline turned down Darren's offers to help as she finished tidying up, then looked at Hazel and Sampson sleeping soundly beside each other in Hazel's basket on the floor.

'I think everyone's had a long day,' she said, looking out of the windows as dusk fell over Sycamore Park. The sky was still clear, stars starting to appear, but the wind had got up, sending flurries of leaves racing up and down the paths. There was no denying that autumn was here, fighting off the early vanguard of winter by the skin of its teeth. In a couple of weeks, the trees would have been reduced to skeletons, and Madeline would be faced with wondering what she would do when Angela decided to return. For a while she had forgotten all about her absent landlord, but her brief tenure was more than halfway done.

She was going to miss it, she realised.

Madeline cut two slices of walnut-topped cheesecake, then poured a glass of wine for herself and a squeezed juice for Darren, before helping him to a window seat where they sat together, looking out over the park.

'So,' he said, 'Do you think it was your ex who broke the window?'

Madeline sighed. 'It has to be,' she said. 'Who else might have done it?'

'What are you going to do?'

'Well, I'm going to wait until I've calmed down, then I'm going to find out the truth. I don't care what he thinks about my petition. He has no right to go damaging the café. And what if we hadn't found Hazel?'

'Perhaps you should call the police?'

'I don't think they would do anything, do you?'

Darren shrugged. 'Probably not.'

Madeline put her hands over his. 'Thank you for getting Hazel out of that tree,' she said.

Darren shrugged. 'It was Ivy's idea. I was just at the top of a greater effort. Rescuing cats is a team game, after all.'

Madeline smiled. 'Thank you anyway.'

She realised she was leaning forwards, moving closer to him. Darren moved forwards too, and suddenly they were leaning over the table, their faces close. Madeline heard Hazel meow, wanting to go out, and hesitated just a moment, but she wouldn't be denied. She leaned forwards a little more, and their lips brushed.

It was Darren who pulled back. Madeline frowned, but Darren lifted his sleeve and gave her a sheepish grin.

'I'm afraid I put my arm in the cheesecake,' he said.

While she wanted to confront Rory, she didn't actually know where he lived now, and while she probably could have hunted him down, she thought it better to channel her energy into something more productive. On a rainy Wednesday afternoon, she left Ruby to look after the handful of customers, took a large umbrella and walked around town, collecting her petition sheets. Then, armed with a bag full of cumulative rage in written form, she headed for the council office.

A junior official who worked on the management team for Sycamore Park was happy to see her.

'As you can see from some of the notes,' Madeline said, 'in addition to more than eight thousand signatures against the car park, there are about a hundred complaints about the shady process of Snide and Company in other car parks around Brentwell.'

To her surprise, the junior official just nodded.

'I got wheel-clamped outside the chemist on Border Street,' she said. 'Turns out you're supposed to park facing outwards. I mean, what a stupid rule. And it only says it in the fine print at the bottom of the Pay and Display sign.'

Not really expecting the council to do anything, Madeline took some advice Darren had given her, and went to one of Brentwell's local radio stations. They seemed even more interested in the situation, and promised to broadcast the problems with Snide and Company as well as talking about the petition in an upcoming news segment.

Madeline walked back to the café, feeling a sense of achievement. When she arrived, however, Ruby was sitting at an outside table, looking glum. The café was empty, the park quiet as evening rapidly approached.

'Are you alright?' Madeline asked, sitting down across from Ruby. 'We didn't get an unexpected bus tour roll in, did we?'

Ruby looked up, a tear in her eye. 'I've got some bad news,' she said.

'Really? What?'

'I have to hand in my notice.'

'You … have to … what?' Madeline wanted to tell her that she couldn't leave, but Ruby was still a student, a young woman at the beginning of her life. Their time working together had always been likely to be short-lived.

'I'm sorry. I really loved working here. It's just that someone saw me playing cricket last weekend, someone from the EWCB.'

'The what?'

'The English Women's Cricket Board. They've chosen me as part of a regional development squad to go on an overseas autumn and winter tour to New Zealand and Australia.'

'Wow, that's fantastic.'

Ruby's glum expression was broken by a smile, like the sun peering among clouds. 'Yeah, it kind of is.'

'You have to go.'

'I know. And after that there's the possibility of a professional contract with one of the regional league sides. I have to finish my studies part time.'

'Ruby, that's amazing. What did your dad say?'

'Well, after he muttered some random statistic or other, he started to cry. Then he hugged me and told me I was the next Rachel Heyhoe-Flint. I had to look her up on the internet.'

'I'm so proud of you.'

Ruby shrugged. 'I mean, after this tour, I'll be back in England, and I might be able to do a few hours a week. The women's cricket league doesn't start until the spring, and I don't think the contracts are full time, so … I might be able to work here for a bit.'

'That would be great,' Madeline said, before realising what she had said, and remembering that it was unlikely she would be here then, either. At the thought of leaving, she felt a sinking feeling in her chest.

'So I just thought I'd better let you know.'

'I think it's brilliant. Obviously I'll miss you, but it's such a great opportunity.'

'Thanks. By the way, your ex-boyfriend showed up about half an hour ago.'

'Really?'

Ruby scowled. 'I gave him a piece of my mind.'

'You did?'

'Yeah. He reckons he had nothing to do with the window. He said he was in London last weekend on a business trip, and didn't get back until Monday. He showed me the train tickets and then started flicking through pics on his phone to prove it.' Ruby rolled her eyes. 'What a clown. He had all these dumb selfies in front of Big Ben, doing all these stupid faces. Honestly, what a total muppet. It looks like his alibi checks out though.'

'If he didn't do it, then who?'

'Actually, Lizzie stopped by this afternoon, and it turns out the library has CCTV cameras, one of which faces across the library courtyard towards the café. She said if we go over there tonight, she'll ask one of the computer guys to play it back and see if it picks up who threw the rock.'

Madeline stood up. 'Let's go,' she said. 'Let's go and find out who it was.'

'Right now?'

'Right now. We'll take them a couple of slices of cake to say thanks.'

Lizzie, the blonde-haired young librarian, was all too happy to take them upstairs to a back room, where Lawrence, an older computer technician with speckled grey hair asked them to sit on a ring of chairs around his oversized computer screen.

'We have three cameras,' he told them., 'One that covers the library floor and the counter, one that faces out of the main lobby, and one that faces across the front courtyard towards your café. After Lizzie told me what happened, I had a look back over the digital footage, and this is what I found.'

He clicked a button and a grainy, odd-angled view of the front of the library appeared. The camera was high up on one wall, looking down across the library's entrance. In the top back corner, beyond a line of trees, the side of the Oak Leaf Café was poking out. You couldn't see the entrance, but you could see the side wall with the windows that faced the park.

'As you can tell,' Lawrence said, 'this doesn't show the broken window, so I think you'd struggle to use this as part of a court case. However, take a look at this.'

He pressed a button and the video playback began to reverse. People walked backwards at rapid speeds and the glow of the sun weakened as it retreated back below the horizon. Darkness fell in reverse, until Lawrence paused the video again.

'Wait,' he said.

The café area was dark, the video lit only by a single streetlight outside the library. A figure walked past, clearly a woman, but walking unsteadily on high-heeled shoes.

'It appears that she's had a little too much to drink,' Lawrence said.

The figure, stumbling from side to side, walked across the courtyard and disappeared into the gloom. Then, a few seconds later, a light flashed on outside the café, illuminating the figure standing outside.

'That's the outside light,' Madeline said. 'It has a motion sensor.'

'Watch her now,' Lawrence said.

The figure stumbled against one of the outdoor tables. Then, leaning against it, she pulled off one of her shoes, lifted it like a club, then charged out of sight around the corner. She appeared again a couple of seconds later, the shoe still lifted over her shoulder. A couple more times she disappeared from sight, then finally, putting the shoe down on the tabletop she hobbled to the side of the café and appeared to pick something up off the floor. With the object in her hands, she disappeared around the side of the café again.

When she returned, she picked up her shoe and put it

back on. As she started to walk, however, it became clear the heel had broken off, and she disappeared into the gloom, walking with an exaggerated limp that would have made any pirate proud.

'TikTok will go crazy over this,' Ruby said. 'Especially if we put it to some decent music.'

'Do you know that person?' Lizzie asked, turning to Madeline.

Madeline stared at the video as Lawrence wound it back to before the woman's unprovoked attack. She thought about it for a few seconds, then nodded. 'I'm pretty sure I do,' she said. 'That was my former therapist, Doctor Janine Woodfield. She also happens to be my ex-boyfriend's fiancée.'

'It looks like she bashed the window in with her shoe then pushed a rock through the gap to make it look like that was how she had done it,' Ruby said. 'What a total fiend.'

'She has plenty of motive to dislike me,' Madeline said. 'I'm her fiancé's ex-girlfriend, I cancelled my sessions with her, and she also has this chip on her shoulder about our school days, when she claims I bullied her. It's not true, by the way. We didn't really have much interaction. I probably could have been nicer to her, but I just kind of ignored her like everyone else.'

'This alone might not be enough to have her convicted of anything, but I imagine the police would be interested,' Lawrence said.

'Let me think about it,' Madeline said.

Having copied the CCTV footage onto a USB, Madeline

and Ruby thanked Lawrence and Lizzie and headed back to the café.

'What are you going to do?' Ruby asked.

Madeline just smiled. 'I'm still thinking about it,' she said.

28

HAPPY AUTUMN, EVERYONE

Jonas was sitting in front of the TV when he got home, watching the news, an excited look on his face.

'You've got them,' he said, pointing to the news segment, which, on first look, appeared to be something boringly political. 'Trading Standards have opened an investigation into Snide and Company for shady business practices.'

'Really?'

'They've received too many complaints, that they can no longer ignore them.'

'That's great news. Hopefully something will actually get done about it.'

'How was your day?'

Madeline just smiled. 'Oh, okay, I suppose.'

The next morning, it didn't take long to find what she was looking for. While weeding the verge around the front of the café, she found the broken heel of Janine's shoe lying in the grass, covered by fallen leaves. The net, should she wish it, would soon close.

However, she was feeling a little more charitable than that.

She called and booked an urgent appointment. Luckily, Janine had an opening that afternoon.

'Please come in,' Janine told her, looking somewhat more flustered than before. Perhaps she had been watching the news.

Janine's office looked different. The shelves, previously teeming with books and ornaments, had been cleared, just lines of dust remaining. Boxes stacked behind Janine's desk revealed their overloaded contents, flaps open to reveal the hurriedly packed remains of a business.

'Are you going somewhere?' Madeline asked.

'Yes, yes,' Janine said. 'My fiancée and I have decided to move overseas for a while.'

Madeline tried to maintain a normal level of surprise. 'Oh, how exciting. May I ask where?'

'Australia. Just for … the foreseeable future.'

'Any particular reason?'

Janine shrugged. 'I suppose neither of us are fans of the English weather. Particularly at this time of year.'

Outside the window, the distant treetops of Sycamore Park looked beautiful. Madeline just shrugged; she supposed some people were never happy.

'Oh dear. I suppose I'll have to find another therapist. Although, I think you managed to cure me pretty well.'

Janine looked like she wanted to be somewhere else. 'That's good, I suppose. Was there anything you specifically wanted to talk about?'

Madeline frowned. 'Well, there was something. I had a

weird dream the other night. It felt like I was looking through a camera angle from above the library doors, down at my café. And in my dream I saw a figure of a woman, and she was attacking my café in a fit of rage. And then—in my dream—I found a piece of the shoe used in the attack.' She looked up at Janine, whose brow was beaded with sweat. 'What do you think it could mean? Do you think … the figure in the dream could have been me?'

'Ah, maybe, yes, who knows? Perhaps you … have issues?'

Madeline frowned. 'And the weirdest thing is, that when I got to the café the next morning, there was actually a broken window.' She smiled and gave a brief, dry chuckle. 'How strange is that?'

'Yes, very strange. Very strange indeed.'

'Do you think I'm insane? I mean, I'm scared to look around, in case … I find the piece of the shoe. That would mean that what I dreamed was … real. Wouldn't it?'

Janine just looked uncomfortable. She still hadn't sat down.

'By the way, how are the wedding plans going?'

'Ah, so-so.'

'I heard that the community centre on Porter Street looks lovely at this time of year. It might be perfect for a reception.'

Janine gave an absent frown. 'There are rumours that it's haunted.'

'Oh, I wouldn't worry about that. But maybe Australia would be much nicer.'

'Yes, yes, maybe. So, was there anything else?'

Madeline just shook her head. For a moment she let her smile drop as she stared at Janine. 'I hope you and Rory are very happy,' she said. 'And no hard feelings, okay?'

Janine just gave her an uncomfortable look before turning away. 'Yes, right, well, I think we can waive the fee for today's session.'

'That's very kind of you. I can see myself out.'

She turned and walked out through the door, giving a little whistle as she went. After all, it was a beautiful day.

They had a grand party at the café for Ruby's last day. Madeline made the invite open, asking everyone to bring a dish and their families. The entire Morton Road cricket team showed up, most of them with wives and kids. Daniel came with Milady, Pete came with his wife and daughter. Lizzie, Lawrence, and a few other library staff showed up, as did Tom with his fiancée, Jennifer. Milady enjoyed running around with Jennifer's little dog, Bonky, although Hazel and Sampson seemed a little disgruntled at being shut into the kitchen to avoid being trampled.

Also in attendance were Madeline's father, her brother, Eric, and his fiancée Amy, but notable for their absence—even though Madeline had sent a cheeky text invite, just to be nice—were Rory and Janine. In a spare moment, Madeline had a quick stalk online and found that Rory's social profiles had finally been updated with a photograph of two hands entwined, engagement rings visible, boarding passes for a flight to Australia placed artistically underneath. Most of the comments were kind and congratulatory, although one anonymous poster had written: Does this mean you'll be leaving our car parks alone?

Not everything was perfect, however. The council, forced by public opinion—not to mention a criminal investigation of the company involved—to drop its plans to privatise the theatre car park, was smarting at the loss of its chance to make money, but their alternative response had been much more passive. Instead of CCTV cameras, narrower spaces and fines for going over the lines, they had installed a donations box by the car park's main entrance.

As the party began to wane late in the evening, Madeline found herself outside, sitting alone at one of the tables. Evenings were drawing in now, the sun setting at around six o'clock. Many of the giant sycamore trees were now half bare, leaves piling up around their bases, others fluttering through the air with each gust of wind. In a couple of weeks many would be bare, the rain would be more frequent, and perhaps customers would become few and far between. Dan would be working a token three nights a week, Pete's van would only be there on weekends, and without Ruby, Madeline felt a tingle of impending loneliness. Rather than fear it, however, she found she was almost welcoming it. Perhaps she could find time to do other things: to read more books, perhaps take a course in something, maybe learn a craft in her free time. Rather than fearing the unknown as she might have once done, she had shed her insecurities in the most unlikely of places: a few short miles from home.

Angela had called earlier, from a hotel in Nepal. Apparently her and Greg were having such a great time that they'd decided to extend their trip by a few months, and wouldn't now return until May. Would Madeline be happy enough staying on as manager until then?

Madeline had agreed without hesitation, her brain taking a moment to catch up with her mouth. The decision had already been there, before Angela's question. Saying yes had been just a formality.

It might not last forever, but then nothing would. But for now, Madeline was happy, already thinking about what she could do at the café to make Halloween special, and after that of course, there would be Christmas to think about. The weeks had a tendency to fly by. She remembered Sycamore Park's Christmas lights as a child. They had been beautiful, and now she would be right in the middle. She was already tingling with excitement.

'Hey. Sorry I'm late.'

At the sound of the familiar voice, Madeline smiled before she looked up. Darren limped out of the dark, a bag over his shoulder. He was off the crutches and the cast had been removed, but his ankle was still a little sore.

'How did it go?' Madeline asked as he sat down.

Darren nodded. 'Good. The poor dear was frantic, thought her doggie was going to die. It had swallowed a plastic band which had got caught in its gut. A bit messy to sort out, but he'll be fine. Shame to waste a Sunday, but the look in her eyes when I told her little Barny was going to be fine made it worth it.'

'Aren't you the only vet who does weekend callouts?'

'In this area. For dogs and cats, at least.'

'And you said you'd only become a vet to please your grandmother.'

Darren glanced up. 'And I know she'd be smiling at me right now. Another happy customer. Another lonely old lady who'll be a little less lonely for a few more years.'

'I think you're doing a great job.'

'As are you. I overheard a couple of customers talking about your blondie crumble cake in the waiting room yesterday.'

Madeline laughed. 'It was supposed to be a white chocolate brownie but I didn't put enough egg in, and it fell apart. I kind of held it together with icing, but I made up the name on the spot.'

'That's how you've got to do it, sometimes. Would you like to take a walk?'

'Sure. Can you?'

Darren lifted his leg and wiggled his foot. With a smile, he said, 'I have eighty-percent mobility. That's pretty good, isn't it?'

Madeline took his arm as they walked up the path towards Big Gerry's plaza. Standing in the middle of the mural that Pete had designed, Darren pointed through the trees, past where a streetlight was yet to blink on.

'Look, you can see the moon.'

Madeline smiled. 'Feels like winter's coming, doesn't it?'

'Not quite yet, but we're on the way, aren't we?' His fingers closed over hers. For a moment she felt a tug as he leaned on his bad foot, then he righted himself.

'Ouch. Still a little tender, I think.'

Madeline leaned her head on his shoulder. He was taller than her, but not by much. His head tilted to rest against hers.

'I'm glad I met you,' he said.

'Happy autumn,' Madeline replied. 'I'm glad I met you, too.'

'What do you want for Christmas?'

'A rest.'

'Yeah, me too. How about we take one together?'

Madeline's heart wouldn't behave. She waited a few seconds before saying, 'Sounds good.'

Darren slowly turned until he was facing her. Then, holding both her hands in his, he leaned forwards.

Moonlight shone down on them. A flutter of leaves fell all around. Madeline felt her lips touch Darren's, and for now, whatever else the world held for them, it was on hold. There was only this moment.

And it was really rather pleasant indeed.

END

ACKNOWLEDGMENTS

Many thanks as always go to those who helped with this book. Jenny Avery for her incredible knowledge and eye for detail, Elizabeth Mackey for the cover, and Paige Sayer for proofreading. And as always, to my muses, Jenny Twist and John Dalton.

Finally, for those of you who support me via Patreon, thanks very much. In no special order: Donna Askins, Mike Wright, Rosemary Kenny, Jane Ornelas, Ron, Gail Beth Le Vine, Sharon Kenneson, Jennie Brown, Leigh McEwan, Janet Hodgson, and Katherine Crispin.

And for everyone who's Bought me a Coffee recently: Sonia Finch, Joeann Davis, Allen from the US, Donna Askins, Vicky B, Sherie Williams Ellen, Hairbender, Randall Balsmeyer, Peter Jaspers-Fayer, Sam Cleeve, Cazuma, Patsy Mcclure, Brinda, GreyCynic, Monica Demmerle, Amy Thay, Cesar Sandoval, Ann Chesterton, Nova Kay, Someone, Jennie B, Mary, Richard Herndon, Claire, Ian Yates-Laughton, Jim Naughton, Rowan Anderson, Andrea Richards, Malcolm from Canada, Elizabeth M. Dykes, Rachel G, Keith Turner, Sheri

Bellefeuille, Niall Nicolson, Amelie Eva, Paul M, Laurie Jones, Aileen MacKinnon, Att, Irena, Michael Fidler, Lindsay G Cowan, Spyke, Rosemary, Marianne, Denise Nicholson, Janet, and Christine Henderson. Thank you. Your support means so much.

Last and not least, to all my readers. Thank you for supporting my books and I look forward to bringing you the next book!

CPW

September, 2023

ABOUT THE AUTHOR

CP Ward is a pen name of Chris Ward, the author of the dystopian *Tube Riders* series, the horror/science fiction *Tales of Crow* series, and the *Endinfinium* YA fantasy series, as well as numerous other well-received stand alone novels. In addition, he writes the critically acclaimed *Slim Hardy Mysteries* under the name of Jack Benton.

Autumn at the Oak Leaf Cafe is the fourth book in the Warm Days of Autumn series.

Expect more soon …

Chris would love to hear from you:
www.amillionmilesfromanywhere.com
chrisward@amillionmilesfromanywhere.net